FUGITIVE TRACKDOWN

SANDRA ROBBINS

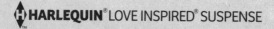

HARLEQUIN® LOVE INSPIRED® SUSPENSE

Recycling programs
for this product may
not exist in your area.

LOVE INSPIRED BOOKS

ISBN-13: 978-0-373-44649-0

Fugitive Trackdown

Copyright © 2015 by Sandra Robbins

www.Harlequin.com

Printed in U.S.A.

"You don't have to be brave for me, Claire."

Claire glared at Adam. "I wasn't trying to be brave. I thought I could do it."

He quirked an eyebrow and smiled. "Whatever you say."

Before he could take a step out of the cabin, a rush of air exploded next to his head, and wood splintered on the door facing. Claire screamed and buried her head in his shoulder as he staggered backward and kicked the door closed.

Another bullet struck the front door, and Adam fell to the floor on top of Claire. He heard her sob and felt her body tremble as he continued to shield her from the gunfire that shattered the cabin windows and streaked over their heads.

Adam had never felt so helpless in his life, but there was no way he could make it outside to confront their attackers without being shot down. His mind raced to find a solution as the barrage grew heavier, but nothing came to mind.

He and Claire were at the mercy of someone who wanted them dead, and they might very well succeed at their mission.

All he could do at the moment was lie still and try to protect Claire and hope that no stray bullet found its mark.

Sandra Robbins is an award-winning, multipublished author of Christian fiction who lives with her husband in Tennessee. Without the support of her wonderful husband, four children and five grandchildren it would be impossible for her to write. It is her prayer that God will use her words to plant seeds of hope in the lives of her readers so they may come to know the peace she draws from her life.

Books by Sandra Robbins

Love Inspired Suspense

Final Warning
Mountain Peril
Yuletide Defender
Dangerous Reunion
Shattered Identity
Fatal Disclosure

The Cold Case Files Series

Dangerous Waters
Yuletide Jeopardy
Trail of Secrets

Bounty Hunters Series

Fugitive Trackdown

Visit the Author Profile page at Harlequin.com.

Now faith is the substance of things hoped for,
the evidence of things not seen.
–Hebrews 11:1

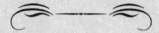

Dedicated to Scott,
who never tires of my endless questions about police procedures

ONE

There hadn't been any movement inside the cabin for the past hour. Claire Walker pulled her coat tighter to ward off the chill of the October night and peered around the tree trunk where she'd decided to conduct her surveillance of the house.

For perhaps the tenth time, she asked herself what was she thinking. Standing in the woods watching a house was the last thing her fellow teachers at Nashville's Hope Academy would have expected from their shy librarian with the nonexistent social life. But sometimes circumstances call for drastic actions.

Her teeth chattered, and she thought of the big fireplace in the den at her father's house back in Memphis and wished she was there curled up in her favorite blanket in front of a roaring fire. She took a deep breath and shook her head. Wishing had nothing to do with it, however. She was on a mission, and she was determined to carry it out.

She glanced down at the pistol she'd purchased a month ago and tightened her grip on it. Hopefully, she'd be able to remember everything the instructor at the firing range had told her if she had to use the gun. Just the thought of aiming the gun and pulling the trigger made her nauseous, but she could do it if need be. She'd made up her mind—she would do whatever it took to bring in the fugitives who'd skipped bond, leaving her father's bail bond business with serious financial problems. Peter Willis would be the first. And for a good reason. When Peter jumped bail, her father had tracked him down, but Peter murdered him in cold blood.

Her heart pricked, and she blinked back tears. Her father didn't deserve to die like that, and she intended to see Peter Willis brought to justice. After Peter, she'd tackle the next one on the list, then the next. Then she'd decide what she wanted to do. Go back to the cocooned life she'd built for herself in Nashville or take on her father's bail bond business in Memphis and the mountain of debt he'd left behind.

She frowned and shook the thought from her head. This wasn't the time to be thinking about her options. All she needed to do at the moment was to concentrate on capturing Peter Willis, and now she had him. Right inside that cabin. The only problem was she had no idea how she was going to apprehend him.

It had all seemed so simple when she'd mapped out her plans at home. All that had gone up in smoke earlier tonight when another man arrived at the remote cabin before she could take Peter into custody.

Now, instead of a single two-hundred-pound man, she had two to contend with. There was no way she could take both of them by herself. If she could get Peter by himself, she might be able to get him out of there before the other one knew what had happened. She had to be patient and wait for the right time.

To her left a twig snapped, and she jerked to attention. Was someone else in the forest with her? Her heart pounded, and her stomach roiled at the thought that one of the men had slipped from the cabin without her seeing him or that another friend was about to join them. She froze in place and listened, but she heard nothing else.

After a moment she relaxed and directed her attention back to the cabin. There had to be something she could do. But what?

The thought had barely entered her mind when the front door opened, and Peter strolled around the side of the house as if he didn't have a care in the world. He stopped at his car, unlocked the trunk and pulled the lid up. He bent over to peer inside, and Claire knew it was time to make her move.

She bolted from behind the tree and covered the distance between them as quietly as possible. Then she pressed her gun against his back. "Hands in the air, Willis!"

"Wh-what is this?" he said as he raised his hands.

She took a step back but kept the gun trained on him. "It's time to go back to jail. Now turn around."

The light coming from the room inside the cabin lit his face as he turned, and he frowned. "Who are you and what do you want?"

"I'm Claire Walker, the new owner of Walker's Bail Bonds since you murdered my father. I've come to take you back to answer for the crime of murdering an employee of the Second Citizens Bank and to have you charged with killing my father."

A smug smile pulled at his mouth. "Really? You think you can do all that?"

"I know I can. Besides the two murders, I know my

father found out about some other illegal activities of yours, and I intend to find out what they are."

An amused expression lit his face, and he shook his head. "You'd better be careful. What your father found out got him killed."

She pulled a pair of handcuffs from her jacket and took a step toward him. "Turn around and put your hands behind your back," she ordered.

An amused smirk crossed his face. "I don't have any intention of going anywhere with you."

She took a step closer. Her hand shook, and she took a deep breath to calm her nerves. "Oh, yes, you'll go with me. On your own two feet or dragged by me after I shoot you. Your choice."

He threw back his head and laughed out loud. "Shoot me? You don't have it in you to shoot me. Besides, the gunshot would alert my friend inside, and you'd be dead before you could get out of this yard."

She tightened her grip on the gun to hide how her hands were shaking and cleared her throat. "You don't scare me."

He took a step toward her and scowled. "You'd better be scared because I don't have any intention of going anywhere with you."

She backed up a step and inhaled a deep breath.

Suddenly she felt the nudge of something against her back. She glanced around to see the man who'd arrived earlier standing behind her with a gun pressed between her shoulders.

Claire whirled around, but the man was quicker. He grabbed her pistol, wrenched it from her hand and hit her across the face with his gun. The handcuffs flew out of her hand as she fell to the ground. She lay there with her head pounding as if a freight train were passing through it. Before she could catch her breath, Peter reached down, kicked the handcuffs and her gun away, and hauled her to her feet. A sharp pain shot up her leg from her ankle, and she groaned.

The man holding the gun glanced at Peter. "Who is she?"

"Her name is Claire Walker," Peter said. "She's the daughter of that old bail bondsman we took care of a few weeks ago."

Claire twisted from the man's grip and tried to fight back the tears at hearing her father referred to in that way, but it was no use. Before she realized what she'd done, she turned to Peter and slapped him across the face. "How dare you talk like that about my father? He was a good man, and he gave you a chance to stay out of jail until your court date. And how did you repay him? You killed him! I intend to see you spend the rest of your life in jail."

Peter rubbed his cheek where she'd hit him and doubled up his fist. Claire cringed from the blow she knew was about to come. He pulled his arm back, and then lowered it as he laughed. "I don't think you'll talk so big without your gun," he taunted. "Now I want you to answer some questions for me."

"What?"

Claire tried to inch away from him, but he reached out and grabbed her by the arm. "Oh, like who else knows you were coming here tonight?"

She tried to pry his fingers from her arm with her free hand, but it was no use. She glared at him. "I don't have to tell you anything."

The two men looked at each other, and Peter tightened

his grip. "I'll ask you one more time. Who else have you told about your suspicions that I had something to do with your father's death?"

Claire ignored the pain shooting up her arm and took a deep breath. "Let go of me."

Peter smiled and relaxed his grip. "Well, it seems like you're not going to cooperate. I think we can handle that okay." He glanced at his partner. "I think it's time for our visitor to disappear."

Fear curled in Claire's stomach, and she darted a glance at each of the men. "Wh-what do you mean?"

The man holding the gun laughed. "It means we're the only two leaving here. The only thing that remains to be decided is where that leaves you."

Claire swallowed the bile that poured into her mouth and tried to speak. "What are you going to do?"

Peter shrugged and glanced at the other man. "Kill her. We can't let her run to the police."

Claire tried again to pull free from Peter's hold, but she couldn't. "No, don't do that. Just let me go, and I won't tell anyone I found you," Claire screamed.

Peter released her with a shove. "Oh, really?" he said. "Somehow I don't think I can believe you."

The man holding the gun aimed at her again, but before he could fire, a bullet hit the edge of the roof and ricocheted off a shingle. He spun around and fired into the forest in the direction the bullet had come from. Two more shots kicked up dirt at his feet. Stunned, Claire dropped to the ground and crawled out of the line of fire toward the far side of Peter Willis's car.

Peter climbed into his car and called over his shoulder "Let's get out of here!"

"What about her?"

"Leave her. We've got to go."

Another bullet whizzed past the car. The man who'd been about to shoot Claire ducked and ran toward his car parked in front of the cabin. Desperate to stop them, Claire tried to push to her feet, but a sharp pain in her ankle shot up her leg. All she could do was groan and sink back to the ground. She landed flat on her stomach.

Both cars roared out of the yard, and Claire watched helplessly from her prone position as the taillights disappeared in the darkness. She pounded her fists into the ground. "No!"

She heard running footsteps, and then someone crashed out of the forest and stopped next to her. "Are you all right?" She could hear concern in the man's question.

Claire flattened her palms on the ground and tried to sit up. "I—I think so. Thanks to you."

"Let me help you." He leaned down, gripped her arm and helped her sit up.

"Thank you again," she said. "If it hadn't been for you…" The words froze in her throat, and she stared up at the last person in the world she would have expected to meet outside a cabin in rural Mississippi.

"Adam? What are you doing here?"

Adam Knight released Claire, blinked and then shook his head. An angry growl came from his throat, and he bent over her until their noses almost touched. "Me? I think the question is what are *you* doing here?"

Claire scooted a few inches away and propped her hands on her hips. "I was trying to bring Peter Willis back to Memphis. He killed my father."

Adam's eyes grew large. "What?"

"You heard me. My father posted his bail, Willis left town and my dad went after him. Then Willis killed him. Now, what about you?"

"I was after the other guy, James Lester. The company that posted his bond hired the Knight Agency to bring him in after he jumped bail on an attempted murder charge."

"Well, your guy got away, too."

"I know that, Claire, but I still don't understand why you thought you could bring a guy like Peter Willis in by yourself. If you needed help, why didn't you call me?"

Claire sniffed and shook her head. "As if I'd ever ask you for anything, Mister Big-Time Bounty Hunter. Besides, I couldn't afford your fees."

Adam turned his back on Claire, raked his hand through his hair and muttered under his breath before he faced her again. "Claire, you've been my sister's best friend since middle school, you practically grew up at our house and you know my family owns the biggest fugitive recovery group in Memphis. We wouldn't have charged you anything. Why didn't you come to us?"

Claire doubled her fists and pounded them against the ground. "Because I didn't want to see you, that's why."

He inhaled a deep breath and attempted to control the anger rising inside him. "You didn't want to see me? Then what about Jessica? You could have called her. She would have helped you."

"Because I knew Jessica was busy on another case. Besides, this is my problem. I can take care of it by myself."

He chuckled and shook his head. "Like you did tonight?"

She pounded the ground again with her fists. "Oh,

that remark is so like you. You never miss an opportunity to let me know what your opinion is of me."

He glared down at her. "So we're back to that again. I'm sorry I caused you problems years ago, but I only wanted to save you a boatload of grief. That has nothing to do with what happened tonight. Your pride almost got you killed."

"It wasn't pride. It's just that I don't like to be reminded of what a fool I was to think I saw something in you that wasn't there."

He gave a short gasp and swallowed hard. "I'm sorry you feel that way. Contrary to what you think, I've always admired you a lot. But I don't see any reason for us to be discussing what happened between us years ago. Don't you understand what I just said? You were almost killed tonight. If I hadn't been following James, they would have shot you without giving it a second thought."

She bit down on her lip and sighed. "I know, and I do appreciate your help. It's just that everything has been so difficult since my dad died. I don't know what I'm going to do."

"I'm sorry." He wanted to say more, but he knew his sympathy was the last thing in the world she wanted at this this moment. Instead he held out his hand to her. "We need to get out of here. Let me help you up."

She hesitated a moment before she reached for his hand. With a groan she pushed to her feet. He held on to her for a moment. "Can you stand on your own?"

She nodded. "I think so."

Adam released her hand, and she took a tentative step. Then a low moan escaped her throat, and she lurched sideways. She clawed at the air in an effort to regain her balance, but it was no use. She toppled straight into Adam's arms.

It happened so quickly Adam didn't have a chance to react. One moment he was yelling at Claire for taking on a job she obviously wasn't qualified for, and the next he had scooped her up into his arms. He gazed down into her face and saw her bite down on her lip.

"Are you in pain?" She nodded but didn't say anything. He stood there a moment, trying to decide what to do, and then she shivered. "Are you cold?"

"Yes."

He turned and walked around the cabin to the front door. It still stood open. He carried Claire into the house, kicked the door closed behind them and looked around. A fire warmed the room, and a couch faced the fireplace. He set her on the sofa and knelt in front of her.

"Let me take a look at that ankle."

She flinched from his touch as he began to pull her boot off. "No, really. I'll be okay. I just need to get home."

He stared up at her. "Why do you always have to be so independent? You may need to go to the hospital. I need to see what your ankle looks like."

She exhaled and leaned back against the cushions. "Then do it. I don't think I'm in any condition to fight you right now."

He tried to hide the smirk that pulled at his lips. "It's good to see you can be sensible sometimes."

Adam slipped her boot and sock off her foot. He frowned and sucked in his breath at the sight of how swollen the ankle was. He touched it lightly, and she groaned. "That hurt."

He sat back on his heels and stared for a moment before he stood up. "I'm sorry. I think we need to get you to a hospital."

Claire shook her head. "We need to get after those men. I had a hard time finding Peter, and I don't want to lose his trail."

"I'm afraid we already have. We'll have to rethink what's to be done. The first thing is I'd like to talk you into letting us find Willis for you."

"Your sister is my best friend. I'm not going to impose on her family to help me out when I can't pay them."

Adam sat back on his heels and stared at her. "Claire, we would never think you were imposing."

"Maybe not, but I can't do it."

He sighed and rose to his feet. "I will give you credit for one thing, though. You found Willis. A lot of bounty hunters are never able to find the guy they're looking for. How did you know he was here?"

Her face flushed, a sign that his compliment hadn't gone unnoticed, and she smiled. "I remember hearing your dad talking to you one time about being a bounty hunter. He said you had to research your fugitive until you knew everything about him. I found out that Peter likes to gamble in Tunica and that his family had this cabin nearby. I asked around about him and finally spotted him at a blackjack table in one of the local casinos. I followed him back here tonight and was just about to take him into custody when your guy showed up."

Adam pushed to his feet and glanced around the cabin. "Well, we've lost both of them now. But as long as we're inside the Willis cabin, we should take a look around."

Claire started to stand, but she groaned and sank back

to the sofa. "I can't. See if you can find anything that might help us."

He pointed to the room just off the living area. "This looks like it could be his bedroom. I'll look in there."

She nodded and patted the couch. "Okay. I'll wait right here."

Adam walked into the room and looked around. A lamp on a bedside table cast a glow across the room, and he glanced around to see if Peter Willis might have left anything behind. An open suitcase sat on the floor against one wall, and he squatted down beside it. A few rumpled clothes that looked as if they were ready to be laundered lay inside. Rising, he walked across the room to the closet and opened the door. Two pairs of pants and three shirts hung there. One thing was evident. Peter Willis hadn't taken enough clothing for an extended trip.

Adam walked back into the living room and glanced at Claire. She sat up straighter on the couch. "Did you find anything?"

"No. He had very few clothes."

She frowned. "But that doesn't make sense. If he was planning to disappear indefinitely, why didn't he bring enough clothes to last for a while?"

"I don't know. Maybe he had clothes stashed somewhere else." Adam glanced at the coat rack on the wall just inside the door and the leather jacket that hung there. He walked over, rammed his hand into the pocket, and pulled out a cell phone. He held it up for Claire to see. "Well, well. Look what Peter left."

Claire sat up straighter on the couch and motioned for Adam to bring her the phone. "Maybe we can find out where he's been by looking at his recent calls and texts."

Adam nodded and sat down next to Claire on the sofa.

"I was just about suggest that." She scooted closer and watched as he scrolled through the calls. He frowned as he stared at the phone. "There are several calls to a number in the Middle Tennessee area code and more to a number in the Smoky Mountain area in the eastern part of the state. These other ones are all to a number in Memphis, probably his wife."

Claire stared down at the phone for a moment before she glanced up at him. "Why don't you call the ones we don't know and see who answers?"

Adam started to call the first number but stopped. "We can do this later, Claire. Right now we need to get that ankle taken care of." He let his gaze drift over her once more. "Do you think you can stand?"

"I'm sure I can."

She placed her hands on the cushions on either side of her and pushed up. She made it halfway to a standing position before she cried out in pain and toppled forward. Adam caught her before she fell to the floor and scooped her up into his arms once more.

He tightened his grip around her and shifted her in his arms. Then he looked down at her and chuckled. "You don't have to be brave for me."

She glared at him. "I wasn't trying to be brave. I thought it was better."

"No matter what you thought, we need to get that ankle checked out. I'll take you to the hospital in my car. Then I'll get my brother, Lucas, or Jessica to come back with me tomorrow to pick up your car."

"I don't think that will be necessary. I think by tomorrow I'll be able to drive."

He quirked an eyebrow and smiled. "Whatever you say."

Adam glanced around the cabin to make sure he wasn't leaving anything behind before he headed across the room. He stopped at the front door, and Claire reached up and switched off the light. Juggling her in his arms so he could reach the door knob, he turned it and pulled the door open.

Before he could take a step, a rush of air exploded next to his head, and wood splintered on the door facing. Claire screamed and buried her head in his shoulder as he staggered backward and kicked the door closed.

Another bullet struck the front door as Adam landed on the floor with Claire on top of him. In one swift move he rolled over and covered her with his body. He heard her sob and felt her tremble as he continued to shield her from the gunfire that shattered the cabin windows and streaked over their heads.

Adam had never felt so helpless in his life, but there was no way he could make it outside to confront their attackers without being shot down. His mind raced to find a solution as the barrage grew heavier, but nothing came to mind.

He and Claire were at the mercy of someone who wanted them dead, and they might very well succeed in their mission. All he could do at the moment was lie still and try to protect Claire and hope that no stray bullet found its mark.

TWO

Terrified, Claire tried to lie still, but she couldn't control the fear that shook her body. She jammed her fist in her mouth, but it only softened her crying a bit. She closed her eyes and said a prayer as the bullets continued to strike the front door and the window next to it. She cringed beneath Adam as the shattered glass hit the floor.

When would it stop? Surely they had to run out of ammunition at some point.

Adam pressed his mouth to her ear and whispered, "Don't be afraid. You're going to be all right. They should get tired of this soon."

She didn't respond but wondered if he really meant it or if he was only trying to comfort her.

Then just as suddenly as it had started, the shooting stopped. Neither Adam nor Claire moved for a minute or two. Then he slowly raised his head, cocked it to the side and frowned as he listened. "Do you think they're gone?" she asked.

"Maybe," he said. "I'm going to get up and check. Don't move until I get back."

He crawled away from where she lay to the front door

and stopped as he pulled his gun from its holster. Then slowly he reached up, grasped the door knob and pulled the door open. He waited, as if expecting a bullet to strike, but nothing happened. After a minute he crawled out onto the porch and disappeared from her view.

The eerie silence sent new chills through Claire. She listened for any sounds outside but heard nothing. The minutes ticked by without Adam's return, and a feeling of panic began to grow in her mind.

Had their attackers left? If so, where was Adam, and why didn't he come back? A new fear flashed in her mind. What if they had knocked him out? Or worse yet, stabbed him, and he was lying in the yard bleeding to death.

The more she imagined what was happening outside, the more frightened she became. She had to find out where he was.

She crawled to the front door and hesitated a moment before she pushed up on her good leg and peeked out. No sign of Adam. Taking a deep breath, she hobbled onto the front porch and leaned against the railing.

Which way would he have gone? Earlier, Peter's car had been parked on the left side of the house, and she faced in that direction. Holding on to the railing, she hopped on her good foot until she'd reached the far end of the porch, but she couldn't see around the edge of the house. She leaned over the banister and tried to peer around the side of the cabin, but it was no use. Before she could straighten up, a hand clamped down on her shoulder. She screamed and whirled to face her attacker.

Adam reached out and grabbed for Claire as she toppled backward, but she slipped from his grasp and hit the porch with a loud thump. Still holding his gun, he leaned over and glared down at her. "What do you think you're doing?"

Claire grabbed her ankle, massaged it with both hands and gulped a deep breath. He couldn't tell if it was fear or anger behind the look in her flashing eyes. "I was coming to check on you. I was afraid they'd killed you or something."

He tried not to smile at her remark, but it was impossible to keep a straight face. His mouth twitched from a frown into a grin, and he cocked an eyebrow. "Or something? Is that worse than being killed?"

The teasing tone of his voice appeared to pacify her some, and a small smile pulled at the corner of her mouth. She rolled her eyes and swatted at the hand he held out to help her up. "Never mind that. I was coming to check on you."

"Then I suppose I should thank you, but I believe I told you to stay where you were until I returned."

She nodded. "Yes, you did, but I'm sure you remember I've never been very good at taking orders."

He stuck his gun back in his holster and shook his head. "No, you never have been." He squatted down beside her, and his gaze raked her. "Are you all right?"

"I'm fine. Are they gone?"

He nodded. "It looks like it. We can leave now."

She sat up and stared at him. "Do you think Peter and James came back?"

"I suspect they were the ones. Who else would want to shoot us? But this makes no sense. James Lester doesn't have a history of violence. Why now?"

Claire's face warmed, and she stared down at her clasped hands. "It could be because of what I told them."

He leaned closer. "And what was that?"

She took a deep breath. "That my father knew Peter had killed a man and that he was involved in some illegal activities. And I was going to see that he was brought to justice."

Adam's eyes grew large, and his mouth gaped open. "Why would you tell him such a thing?"

"Because it's true, and I intend to do it."

"But, Claire, he was going to kill you because of it, and it looks like they came back to finish the job."

"Maybe they just wanted to scare us. At any rate, they might have gotten tired, or maybe they ran out of ammunition, or they thought no one could have lived through such a barrage. Who knows? But whatever the reason, they're gone now."

Adam sighed, reached down and picked her up again. "We're not going to figure it out right now, so we'd better get you to that hospital. Hopefully this time we can get to the car."

She stiffened as his arms tightened around her. "I really don't need to go to a hospital. If you'll just take me home…"

"Save your breath, Claire," he interrupted. "We're going to the hospital to see what a doctor says. And from the looks of things, you're in no condition to argue with me."

She clamped her lips together and glared at him as he carried her down the porch steps. He glanced around once more before he headed through the forest.

She didn't say anything as he plodded through the thick growth of the woods and ducked under low-hanging branches, but he couldn't help thinking about how close she had come to death tonight. If he hadn't been there, she would now be lying next to the cabin with a bullet in her head.

Adam's arms tightened around her at the thought. She shifted in his arms, and he loosened his grip. She didn't have to say the words aloud. It was almost as if he could read her mind. She might be grateful to him for saving her life, but she would never forgive him for what he'd done. The best thing he could do was go home after she got medical attention and chalk Claire Walker up to one more mistake he'd made in the past.

Claire sat on the edge of the exam table and stared down at the elastic compression bandage on her ankle. A pair of crutches leaned against the edge of the table.

A knock on the wall outside the curtained-off exam cubicle caught her attention and she straightened. "Who is it?"

"Claire, may I come in?" Adam called out.

"Yes."

He pushed the curtain aside and stepped into the small exam area.

"The doctor says you can leave now. Are you ready to go?"

She sighed and nodded. "I guess so."

He frowned at the resignation in her voice and stepped closer. "What's the matter?"

She pointed at the bandage and then the crutches. "How am I going to be able to go after Peter Willis if I can't even walk on my own for at least thirty-six hours?"

He raised his eyebrows and shook his head. "I'd say catching up to Willis is the least of your worries right now. Try to remember you're lucky to be alive."

He walked across the room toward her and reached

out to help her down from the table. She pulled back and grabbed for the crutches. "I can handle this."

He raised his hands and backed away. "Okay, if you say so."

Claire leaned on the crutches as she slid off the table onto her good leg and then slipped the crutches under her arms. Holding her injured ankle up, she took a step toward the door. "See," she said, "I can do it by myself."

He stepped around her and opened the door. "Yeah, I know. You always were an independent kid."

Her knuckles turned white as she tightened her grip on the crutches. "I'm not a kid anymore, Adam."

"I know," he said. "But this decision you made about going after a bail jumper doesn't sound too adult to me."

"Sometimes life can cause you to take desperate measures." She pushed past him and into the hall.

He followed behind as she slowly made her way out of the ER and into the parking lot. Outside the ER door he stepped up beside her and pointed toward his car, which sat underneath one of the streetlights. "I moved the car from the entrance to that spot over there after I got you inside. If you'll wait here, I'll go get it so you won't have to walk with your crutches."

"No need for that. I can make it," she said. She took a deep breath and headed toward the car.

"I don't mind, Claire."

"I know, but I need the practice of using these crutches."

He sighed. "Whatever you say."

She kept her eye on the car as she inched her way toward it. It hadn't seemed so far when she'd first spotted it, but the distance seemed to grow with each step. When she finally reached the car, he held the door for her to climb inside before he closed it and went around to the driver's side.

He glanced at her, but she pretended not to notice and preoccupied herself with finding the radio station she wanted. When she'd settled on one, she turned up the volume and leaned back in her seat. The sound of a Christian rock song filled the car.

Adam didn't say anything until he pulled onto Highway 61 and headed back toward Memphis. Then he reached over and turned the volume down. "Not much traffic tonight."

"No, but the casinos in the area are probably filled," she said.

"I guess so." When she didn't answer, he shook his head. "So much for small talk," he muttered under his breath.

After a few minutes Claire reached over and turned the music up louder than before. After a few minutes she glanced over at him. Every time the drumbeat boomed, he winced. As he rubbed the back of his neck and exhaled, Claire directed an innocent look at him. "Too loud?"

"A bit," he said. She reached over and turned it down some. After a few minutes he twisted the knob to silence the roar of the rock band. "I didn't tell you I called the local police while you were being examined. They sent an officer to the hospital, and I gave him a rundown on everything that happened at the cabin tonight. I had the license number for the car James was driving, and he said he could find out Peter Willis's. They have a BOLO alert out on the two cars and will let me know if they find them."

Claire swiveled in her seat to face him. "Good. Did you tell him my car was on the road back of the cabin?"

"Yes. I told him we'd go back sometime tomorrow to pick it up."

"Good." She turned up the volume on the radio, closed her eyes and leaned back in her seat.

He sighed and turned it back down. "Claire, I need to talk to you."

"About what?"

"I've been thinking. It might be better if you went to Jessica's house tonight instead of going home."

She sat up straight and faced him. "Why would I want to do that?"

"Because the doctor said you need to stay off your foot as much as possible, and you need to be on those crutches for at least thirty-six hours. Jessica can help you out, and she wants to."

She narrowed her eyes and stared at him. "And how do you know that?"

"Because I called her and told her what happened. She wants you to go there instead of going home tonight."

Claire rolled her eyes and leaned against the headrest. "That's just great. Now I get to listen to my best friend tell me how dumb it was for me to think I could bring a bail jumper in by myself."

Adam shook his head. "She wouldn't do that. She's concerned that you could have been killed tonight."

She sighed and reached down to rub her ankle. "I guess it would be better if I had someone with me tonight. So take me to your sister's apartment, and then you can go home."

He nodded but didn't say anything for a few moments. Then he darted a glance at her. "Jessica said she's hardly heard from you since your father's funeral. Why haven't you been in touch with us?"

She shrugged. "For the past few weeks I've been going over my father's business affairs. It seems he owed a lot of penalties to the courts because of bail jumpers, and he wasn't getting a lot of new business. I've been trying to figure out how I can save his company. I thought even if I couldn't, I would see that Peter Willis was brought in."

"It sounds like you might stay in Memphis. What about your librarian job back in Nashville?"

"I've taken a leave of absence for the remainder of the semester. I thought I could spend the time taking care of all the loose ends with my father's business, but I didn't know how bad things really were for him."

Her words startled him, and he glanced in her direction. "What do you mean?"

She sighed. "It seems business hadn't been too good lately, and he had a lot of clients jump bail. Besides, that new bail bond business in Memphis has given everybody else some stiff competition."

"You mean the Bond Squad?"

"Yes. Do you know them?"

He nodded. "Yeah. They're the ones who hired me to go after James."

"That figures," she snarled. "They can afford to hire the best bounty hunters."

He grinned and glanced at her. "So you admit I'm the best at what I do."

She let out a sarcastic chuckle. "Don't flatter yourself. I wasn't talking about you personally. I meant your family's business. It just happens to be the oldest bounty hunter group in the city, and maybe in the state."

He laughed and shook his head. "The term *bounty hunter* makes people think about some reality show you might see on TV. That's why we call ourselves a fugitive recovery group."

Her eyebrows arched and she chuckled. "Well, call it whatever you want, mister. But you're still a bounty hunter as far as I'm concerned. I don't think your great-grandfather who started the business had any problem with the term."

"I'm sure he didn't." He smiled. "But things have changed since the days when he hunted bail jumpers up and down the Mississippi River. One thing about him, though, he had a philosophy that has been an inspiration to all of us."

"'A man must answer for the crimes laid against him,'" she said. "That's what he always said after taking someone into custody, wasn't it?"

He darted a surprised glance in her direction. "How did you know that?"

"I ought to know it. I've heard Jessica say it plenty of times. Anyway, I'm glad your business is doing well even if mine isn't."

"Claire, I'm sorry things weren't going well for your father before his death, but I meant it when I said I wished you had come to us. If not to me, then Jessica or Lucas. You know we've always thought of you as family."

She turned and stared at him. "Really? Somehow I always got the impression you'd rather I wasn't around."

He squirmed in the seat and straightened his back. "I'm sorry if I made you feel that way."

"It really doesn't matter now. I must have seemed like a silly little girl to you with my crush on my best friend's big brother, but that's all in the past. Let's just drop the conversation. All right?"

"Sure. If that's what you want. I'll take you to Jessica's, then…" He stopped midsentence and stared in the rearview mirror. "I think we've got a problem."

"What kind of problem?"

"I think we're being followed."

Claire looked over her shoulder and out the back window. "You mean by that car behind us?"

"Yeah. They've stayed right with us for several miles."

"Can you tell if it's one of the cars that Peter and James were driving?"

He squinted and stared into the rearview mirror. "Their headlights are too bright. I can't tell anything about the car."

"What should we do?"

"Let's make sure they're really after us." Adam glanced at the dashboard as he let up on the accelerator. The car's speed dropped by twenty miles per hour. "Now we'll see if he's really tailing us. If not, he'll pass."

He watched for a few minutes, but the car made no effort to pass. He dropped the speed lower, but the vehicle remained several car lengths behind them. Claire glanced back and then to Adam. "He's still there."

"I know." Adam pushed the accelerator down, and the car sped away from the headlights that shone through the rear window of his car. As if on cue, the driver behind accelerated and kept the same distance between them. "Seems like he's going to hang with us."

Claire's eyes grew wide. "What now?"

"Try again." He slowed almost to a crawl, but the car still didn't pass. Then without warning, he floored the accelerator, and the car leaped forward.

Claire screamed and gripped the sides of her seat. Adam cast one glance at her before he hunched over the steering wheel and roared toward the lights of Memphis that were just coming into view.

THREE

Claire stared wide-eyed at the speedometer as it inched higher and then looked at Adam. The reflections from the streetlights they roared past cast an eerie glow across his face that sent cold chills up her spine. He glanced in the rearview mirror, and the muscle in his jaw flexed. She turned her head to stare out the back window and swallowed the fear that rose in her throat. The other vehicle sped through the night perhaps two car lengths behind.

Ahead, the lights of Memphis beckoned as they approached the turnoff that would take them toward the eastern part of the city. She bit down on her bottom lip as the tires squealed and they barreled along the exit and onto the city's loop highway.

The car shook, and she wondered how Adam could remain in control of the speeding car, but he appeared to be having no problem. Even this late at night heavy traffic rolled along the expressway. Adam wove in and out of the cars as if they were on a racetrack. Another glance to the rear told her that the other car hadn't given up the chase.

Finally she could keep silent no longer. "Have you

been able to tell if the car looks like either of the ones James and Peter were driving?"

He shook his head. "I still can't tell, but it has to be somebody connected to what happened earlier tonight. Hang on. I'm going to get off this highway."

Claire gasped as the car swerved along the next exit and roared down Poplar Avenue headed east. Claire looked behind, but the car wasn't in view. Traffic was lighter on this street, but that could be expected at eleven o'clock on a weeknight. Adam didn't slow the car as he wedged his way into a line of traffic in the right-hand lane. Then the lights of another car flashed in the distance, and Claire wondered if they'd been spotted amid the vehicles that moved down the street.

"I think he's behind us again," she said.

Adam didn't reply. Instead he made a sharp right turn into the parking lot of an all-night discount store. A flashing sign next to the street advertised a midnight sale, and the area around the store was filled with cars and people standing in line waiting to get inside.

He drove into the parking lot, found a spot between two cars and pulled in. He quickly killed the engine and turned off the lights. From where they sat they had a good view of the street. Several cars drove by, and then one sped by in the direction they'd been traveling.

Adam exhaled a deep breath. "That looks like the car Peter was driving."

"Do you think we've lost them?"

He shook his head. "I don't know, but I hope so. I don't want them finding their way to Jessica's apartment."

With their followers out of sight, Adam started the car again and pulled back onto the street headed toward the interstate they'd been on minutes before. Thirty minutes later he pulled into the midtown apartment complex where his sister lived.

Claire let out a sigh of relief when they parked. "You did a great job of losing whoever was chasing us. In fact, you've done a good job of everything tonight. Thank you for helping me."

He looped his arm over the steering wheel and swiveled in the seat to face her. "The things I've done tonight require the skills I've picked up from the work I do. It's not easy bringing fugitives back to face the court. If they wanted to go to jail, they wouldn't have run away to start with. I hope what you've seen tonight has shown you how foolish it was for you to think you could bring Peter Willis in."

His words stung, and she fought back tears. "I'm glad to see nothing's changed with you. I've always been foolish as far as you're concerned. Now you'll have one more thing to add to your long list of complaints about me."

She pushed the car door opened and tried to step out onto the pavement, but he reached out and grabbed her by the arm. "What do you think you're doing?"

"I'm going to Jessica's apartment."

He shook his head. "Wait a minute, Claire. You need some help."

Before she could protest, he'd jumped from the car and walked around to the open passenger door. He reached into the backseat and grabbed her crutches. Then taking her by the arm, he helped her to her feet and positioned the crutches in place.

Claire braced herself on the supports and took a tentative step, but she staggered. Adam's hand grasped her arm. She tried to jerk free of his grip, but it was no use.

She sighed in resignation. "Okay, you win. These are a bit harder to maneuver than I thought."

He didn't say anything but tightened his hold on her as they slowly made their way into the building and to Jessica's apartment. They stopped outside the door, and Adam pushed the buzzer. The door flew open right away, and Jessica stood there, her dark hair tumbling around her shoulders and her eyebrows pulled down in a worried frown.

"Where have you two been? I've nearly gone out of my mind waiting."

She pulled Claire into the apartment and helped her to the sofa where she dropped down with a groan. "We had a little problem getting here," Claire said.

Jessica looked at Adam. "What happened?"

"I had to lose a tail. I didn't want to bring him straight here."

Claire propped a sofa pillow behind her back and frowned at Adam. "It's a wonder we got here alive at all the way you were driving." She turned to Jessica. "Don't be surprised if your brother decides to take up stock car racing. He's got all the skills."

Jessica's eyes grew wide, and she looked from her brother back to Claire. "What are you talking about?"

Adam waved his had in dismissal. "Claire's exaggerating. I had to outrun a car, so I had to move fast."

Jessica nodded as if she understood before she turned back to Claire. "Adam told me a little of what happened tonight when he called, but I want the whole story. Why were you at a cabin in the Mississippi woods trying to bring in a bail jumper?"

Claire closed her eyes and shook her head. She'd known telling Jessica about her father's failing business and her efforts to keep it afloat was going to be difficult, but there was nothing she could do about it now. "I've been having a hard time ever since my father's death," she began.

For the next few minutes she related the problems she'd discovered about her father's murder, fugitive bail jumpers, penalties that had accumulated from the courts and how she had decided the only way to save her business was to go after some of the fugitives herself.

Jessica didn't say a word until she finished, then she reached out and grasped Claire's hand. "Why didn't you tell me this? We would have helped you."

"It's not your family's responsibility to take care of my problems. Besides, I thought if you can do it, so can I."

Jessica arched an eyebrow and regarded Claire with a skeptical look. "You're forgetting I was a police officer before I went to work in my family's business. I've had training that you haven't. You could have been killed tonight."

"I couldn't ask you or your family for help. I felt like I needed to do it on my own."

Jessica pursed her lips and shook her head. "You've always been too independent, Claire. There are times when a person needs help."

"That's what I told her," Adam said.

Jessica glanced up her brother and smiled. "Then I'm sure you'll be glad to help her."

"Oh, no," Claire interrupted. "He's already done enough tonight."

Jessica pushed to her feet as if she hadn't heard Claire and faced her brother. "It looks to me like the guy you're after and Claire's bail jumper are tied together some way.

So if you find one of them, you'll be able to find both of them. Adam, you need to bring these guys in. Then Claire can get paid for Willis. That will be a start toward helping her and toward putting her father's killer in jail."

Claire tried to push up from the sofa, but she couldn't. "Jessica, listen to me. I don't want Adam to help me. I can do it myself."

Jessica ignored her. "I would do it, but I'm leaving in the morning for Louisiana to pick up a guy down there. Lucas won't be back from Illinois until the day after tomorrow. So that leaves you, Adam. You're the only one who can do this."

Adam rubbed the back of his neck and cast a doubtful glance in Claire's direction. "I don't know, Jessica. Claire doesn't want me to help her."

Claire reached out and grabbed her friend's arm. "Jessica, listen to me. I don't need Adam's help."

She smiled down at Claire and then looked back at Adam. "I don't know what happened between the two of you years ago, but it's time you let it go. Claire needs help, and you, Adam, are the only one who can do it."

He didn't say anything for a moment. Then he nodded and glanced down at Claire. "Jessica is right. Whether or not you want any help, you need it. But we're all tired tonight. So get some rest, and we'll talk about this in the morning."

"Good," Jessica said. "Now, you go home and get some sleep. I'll take care of Claire."

They walked to the door, and Adam kissed his sister on the cheek before he stepped into the hall. Jessica closed the door behind him and came back to where Claire sat. "Let's get you to bed. I have the spare bedroom made up for you."

She helped Claire to her feet, and they made their way down the hallway toward the bedrooms. "What time are you leaving tomorrow?" Claire asked.

"I'll have breakfast with you and make sure you can move around before I leave. I don't know what time Adam will be here. But if you can't get to the door, he can let himself in with his key."

They entered the bedroom, and Claire smiled at the nightgown Jessica had laid out on the bed for her. She dropped down on the side of the bed and smiled up at her friend. "Thank you, Jessica. It's good to be here with you."

Jessica squatted down and took Claire's hands in hers. "Although we've been friends since middle school, I've never pushed you to tell me what happened between you and Adam. I know you don't like him, but he's really a wonderful person. The problem is, he's never thought of himself that way. I don't think you have, either, but I can't stand to see two people I love continuing to holding some kind of grudge from years ago. I hope you can reach the point where you can let it go."

Tears formed in Claire's eyes and she nodded. "I hope so, too."

Jessica sighed and pushed to her feet. "Do you need me to help you get ready for bed?"

"No, I'll be okay with my handy crutches. Thanks again."

"I'll get one of my robes and bring it back for you."

"Thanks, Jessica."

Jessica covered Claire's hands and squeezed them before she left the room. Claire watched her go and thought about what she had said. Could she ever forgive Adam for how he'd hurt her? She didn't know. Her dislike of him had become a part of her, and she didn't know if she could ever wipe it from her mind.

She did have to admit, though, he'd come to her rescue several times tonight. Maybe he did have some good qualities she'd ignored. The question still remained whether or not she could forgive him. Only the future would tell.

Claire sighed and hobbled on her crutches to the window to close the curtains. As she reached for the cord to close them, the lights of a car in the parking lot behind Jessica's apartment caught her eye. She stopped and stared as a car drove slowly past the parked cars of the residents. It didn't stop but moved to the exit and disappeared around the corner of the building.

Claire tightened her fingers around the cord to draw the curtains, but her body seemed frozen in place. The car that had just passed by looked exactly like the car that had zoomed past their hiding place on Poplar Avenue a short time ago. Had the driver waited for them to lead him where Claire was going to stay that night?

"What are you looking at?" Jessica's voice startled her, and she turned to see her friend standing in the doorway.

Claire glanced down at the robe Jessica held and smiled. "I was just closing the curtains."

Jessica stepped into the room and laid the garment on the bed. "I hope you sleep well."

Claire yawned. "I'm sure I will. I don't know when I've ever been so tired."

"Then I'll say good-night."

"Good night, Jessica."

Claire waited until Jessica had left the room before she turned back to the window and stared outside. After a moment she closed the curtain, inched back to the bed and pulled her gun from her purse. She laid it on the bed-side table, changed into the nightgown Jessica had left for her and then crawled into bed. No matter what she'd told Jessica, she knew sleep wouldn't come.

She pulled the covers up to her chin and waited to see what would happen next.

Claire jolted awake and glanced at the bedside clock with its face glowing in the darkened room—2:00 a.m. Despite her good intentions, she'd fallen asleep. She pushed up in bed and raked her hair out of her face.

Her thoughts drifted back to the events of the night, and she shivered. She'd never been so scared in her life, but at least she was alive. Now she needed to get a grip on her emotions. Nothing else was going to happen to-night, so there was no need for her to try to stay awake. She had a busy day ahead of her tomorrow, and she needed some rest if she was going to make it through.

She plumped up her pillow and was about to lie back down when a noise from the direction of the kitchen startled her. It sounded as though a door had opened. She sat up again and strained to hear any other sounds in the apartment. Nothing. Then the creak of footsteps on the floor sent her heart racing.

Someone had entered the apartment.

Claire eased from the bed, slipped into her robe, and grabbed the gun from the bedside table. She stared at the crutches for a moment before she propped one under her left arm. With the gun in her right hand, she limped toward the bedroom door. Once there she propped the crutch against the wall and balanced on her good foot. Then she eased the door open and slid into the hallway.

She stopped and held her breath when the beam of a flashlight pierced the darkness. Now she had no doubt a prowler had entered the apartment.

She slid along the hallway wall until she reached the living room and then reached for the switch to turn on the overhead light. The man was facing away from her, and he pulled something from her purse. He whirled around just as the room lit up. Her bag tumbled to the floor.

"What…?" he snarled.

Claire's heart jumped into her throat at the sight of James Lester with Peter Willis's phone in one hand and a flashlight in the other. She tightened her grip on the gun. "Put it down, Lester."

His gaze dropped to the gun in her hand, and he smirked. "Still trying to play the tough girl, huh? Well, you don't seem too tough to me."

He took a step toward her, and she swallowed. "I'm warning you. Don't come any closer. Put the phone on the coffee table."

He cocked his head to one side and grinned. "And what are you going to do? Shoot me? I don't think you have it in you."

Perspiration beaded her forehead. "Are you willing to chance it?"

He smiled. "I think I am."

Before she could respond, he hurled the flashlight at her. It hit her in the chest, knocking the wind out of her. He rushed forward, grabbed her wrist and tried to twist the gun from her hand.

"No!" she screamed as she struggled against him. The gun jerked in her hand and fired.

James Lester screamed out in pain, and the gun and

the cell phone he had held clattered to the floor. "You've shot me!" he yelled and staggered backward. "You shouldn't have done that!"

She tried to reach her gun, but he lunged again, grabbed it before she could and pointed it in her face. She closed her eyes and waited for him to fire. Before he could pull the trigger, a voice thundered out. "Get away from her!"

His fingers loosened on her arm, and Claire glanced around to see Jessica with her gun aimed at James Lester. "Jessica, thank goodness…"

He growled, grabbed Claire's other arm and pulled her in front of him. His left arm encircled her waist, and his right one, which held the gun, pressed across her chest. She realized she had just become James Lester's shield. "Put your gun down unless you want your friend here to get hurt."

Jessica didn't back off but inched forward. "Let her go."

"No way." James pulled Claire backward toward the kitchen. She glanced down at the floor and noticed the trail of blood he left behind. She tried to claw at his face, but his arm across her chest held her so tightly she could barely move. "I'm leaving, and I'm taking her with me. If I see any cops following me, I'll dump her body out of the car. Do you understand?"

"I understand you're going nowhere but to jail," Jessica said.

"Not today, sweetheart," he replied. "So back off."

They were almost to the back door now, and Claire knew she had to do something. He released the arm around her waist and reached behind him to open the door, and the pressure of his other arm lessened.

In that split second Claire ducked her head and clamped her teeth into his hand. He yelled in agony and hurled her away from him as the gun clattered to the floor. She stumbled forward and fell against one of the kitchen chairs. She looked up in fear as he took a step toward her. "You'll pay for that!"

Jessica appeared in the doorway, her gun pointed at James. "Hands up, Lester."

The look that washed over his face reminded Claire of a cornered animal. He glanced from side to side, then reached for the coffeepot on the counter next to him and hurled it at Jessica. When she ducked, he opened the door and stumbled out.

Before Jessica reached Claire, he had disappeared, and the sound of a car roaring away split the night air. Jessica dropped to her knees next to Claire. "Are you all right?"

She nodded. "I'm fine."

"Then I'm going to see if I can catch him."

"I don't think you will. I heard a car drive off. Peter Willis must have been waiting for him outside."

Jessica rushed out the back door, and Claire lay there for a moment thinking about what had just happened. This was the second time tonight that someone she'd known since childhood had been put in danger because of her. How could they ever forgive her for that?

Claire tightened her grip on the back of the kitchen chair she'd landed against and pulled herself to her full height just as Jessica walked back into the apartment. "He got away, but at least we know who he was. I've called the police, and I've also called Adam. Everybody should be here in a few minutes."

"Why did you call Adam?"

"He would have been angry with me if I hadn't."

Claire groaned. "Now I get to listen to him lecture me again."

Jessica frowned and shook her head. "You need to get over this idea that Adam doesn't like you. He's really quite fond of you."

"I'm sure he is. About as fond as he his of a headache. But anyway, I'm sorry I put both of you in danger tonight. I didn't intend for that to happen."

"We know that, Claire. It's just that we've been doing this kind of work for a long time. You're new to it."

"I may be new, but I'm learning fast. For instance, I know James Lester broke in here to get Peter Willis's cell phone, but he didn't. Those phone numbers must be more important than we thought at first." Claire took a deep breath and hobbled toward the living room door.

"Be careful of your foot, Claire," Jessica called out.

Claire gritted her teeth and took another step. "James Lester was right about one thing. I have to toughen up. I put my best friend and her brother in danger tonight, and I don't want to do it again."

Jessica followed her into the living room and watched as Claire staggered to the couch and took a seat. Claire reached down and picked up the cell phone James had dropped in the struggle.

"At least he didn't get what he came for. Back at the cabin Peter let it slip that James was also involved in my father's death, and I'm determined they're not going to get away with it. There must be something in this phone that's so important they'd risk breaking in here to get it. Now all I have to do is find out what it is."

Jessica dropped down beside her. "How do you expect to do that?"

Claire shook her head. "I don't know yet, but one thing is for sure. The next time I meet up with those two I intend to be ready for them."

FOUR

Jessica opened the door as soon as Adam knocked. Her look of relief at seeing him and the sight of four grim-faced police officers, two uniformed ones and two he knew to be detectives, let him know the break-in Jessica had told him about on the phone had been much worse than she'd let on.

He stepped into the apartment, and Jessica closed the door behind him. His gaze went straight to Claire, who sat on the couch. One of the detectives sat beside her, and the other stood in front of them. The second detective glanced up at Adam, gave a curt nod and directed his attention back to what his partner was saying to Claire.

Adam turned back to Jessica. "On the phone you made it sound like you'd had a prowler. Now I suspect it was something more serious."

She nodded and pulled him to the side of the room. "I'm sorry. I guess it was foolish of me to think I could downplay the whole thing. To be honest, I was scared. Especially when I had my gun cocked to fire, and he pulled Claire in front of him as a shield."

Adam's mouth dropped open, and he stared in disbelief at his sister. "Used her as a shield? I think you'd better tell me the whole story."

Adam listened as Jessica relayed what had happened in her apartment. When she'd finished, he rubbed his hand across his eyes and groaned. "I shouldn't have brought her here."

Jessica gasped. "Why not?"

"Because it put you in danger. I would never have forgiven myself if something had happened to you."

"And what about Claire? Could you have forgiven yourself if something happened to her?"

"Of course I don't want her to get hurt, but you're my sister. I'm supposed to protect you."

Jessica chuckled and shook her head. "You're forgetting I was a police officer. I think I can take care of myself."

"I know you're good at your job, but that doesn't mean I don't worry about you."

Jessica arched an eyebrow. "There's no need to do that."

"You think so, huh? For your information, I do." He glanced toward the detective standing in front of Claire. "That detective keeps looking this way at you, like he's trying to send you some secret message. What's that all about?"

Jessica shrugged and diverted her gaze away from him. "That's Ryan Spencer, my former partner, but I don't have any idea what you're talking about."

Adam studied her for a moment. "Did something happen between the two of you? Something I don't know about?"

She shook her head. "There's nothing for you to concern yourself with."

"Look, Jessica, I know how hard it is for you to let things go, and I can tell you're hiding something from me. Why won't you tell me what it is about this guy that upsets you so? I want to help you if I can."

Her face paled, and she took a deep breath. "It's ancient history. Just like whatever happened between you and Claire."

"Now wait a minute, we're not talking about me."

"Maybe we should be," she said. "You want to make me happy? Then take care of my friend while I'm gone to pick up our latest bail jumper. Since her father was killed, she's kept her distance from me, and I don't like it. If she's avoiding me because of you, I want you to fix it."

He rubbed the back of his neck. "It's not that simple, Jessica."

She directed a somber stare at him. "It doesn't matter. You're my brother, and I'm asking you to protect my friend. She's in danger, Adam, and you may be the only one to help. She practically grew up at our house. If you don't feel like you owe her something, then do it for me."

He looked at Claire, who was still giving her story to the detectives, and noticed how vulnerable she looked sitting beside the seasoned detective. She had almost been killed twice tonight. Those had to have been the worst experiences of her life. And like his sister said, Claire had been a fixture in their home when she was growing up. Even if she hated him now, he owed it to her to see that she stayed safe.

He nodded. "Okay, Jessica. I'll watch out for her. I don't want anything to happen to her, either."

She put her arm around his waist and hugged him. "I know you don't. You're a good guy, Adam. I just hope Claire can come to see that."

"I do, too."

The detective sitting next to Claire stood at that moment, pulled his business card from his pocket and handed it to her. "I think that about does it, Miss Walker. We'll check with the hospitals to see if anyone has treated a gunshot wound, and there's already a BOLO out on Lester and Willis. If you think of anything else, give me a call."

Claire glanced down at the card. "I will, Detective Barnes. There is one thing, though. I'll feel safer when James Lester and Peter Willis are in custody. Would you let me know if you find them?"

"Sure. Give me your cell phone number."

He wrote her number in a small notepad and put it in his pocket before he motioned for the uniformed officers to follow. They trailed him to the door where Jessica met them. She opened it and smiled at Detective Barnes. "Thank you for coming, Mac," she said as the men exited.

"Good to see you again, Jessica," he said. "We still miss you around the station. How's the bounty hunter business?"

She smiled. "It keeps me busy," she replied.

Detective Barnes allowed the uniformed officers to step into the hall before him, but Ryan Spencer stopped beside Jessica. He looked as if he was about to say something, but she bit down on her lip and glanced down at the floor. After a moment he frowned and followed his partner into the hall. Jessica watched them go before she closed the door and came back to where Adam stood.

"Are you okay?" Adam asked. "You seemed a bit aloof with Ryan. Were you uncomfortable seeing officers you used to work with?"

Jessica waved her hand in dismissal. "Didn't bother me at all. I'm glad to be out of the department and working at the Knight Agency now. Which reminds me, you work there, too, and you have a job to do to help Claire find Peter Willis."

He took a deep breath and directed his attention back to Claire, who still sat on the couch. "Yeah, I guess I do."

When he didn't move, Jessica grabbed his arm and led him over to the couch. Claire looked up at them when they stopped. "Adam wants to talk to you," Jessica said. "Since I have to leave so early in the morning, I think I'll try to get some sleep." She glanced at Adam. "You can let yourself out when you and Claire get through talking."

He shook his head. "After what's happened here tonight, I don't feel good leaving you two alone. I'll get a blanket and a pillow out of the hall closet and sleep on the couch for the rest of the night."

Claire shook her head. "There's no need for you to do that."

"I think there is," he said. "Besides, we need to get your car in the morning."

Jessica nodded. "I think your staying here is a good idea."

Claire shrugged. "Whatever you two say. I don't want to cause you any more trouble than I already have tonight. But, Jessica, I want to see you before you leave in the morning."

"You will, and you haven't caused us any trouble. We only want to see that you're safe." Jessica put her hand over her mouth and yawned. "Now if you'll excuse me, I'm off to bed."

Claire's gaze followed Jessica until she disappeared

into her bedroom. Then she turned to Adam. "What do you want to talk to me about?"

"First of all, I want you to know how glad I am that James Lester didn't hurt you tonight."

"Me, too." She blinked from the tears that filled her eyes. "I have to confess I was really scared for a few minutes there."

"I know you must have been, but that's to be expected. After all, you'd nearly been killed earlier. I've had narrow escapes that made me wonder why I wasn't killed."

She tilted her head to the side and stared at him. "Really? I always thought nothing scared you."

"I wish that were true, but it's not. There were times when I was in Iraq that I thought I'd die any moment."

"I never knew that."

He took a deep breath. "Which brings up something I think we need to talk about. That night six years ago when I was home on furlough."

She shook her head and tried to rise. "There's nothing we need to discuss."

He reached out and grabbed her arm. "I think there is. I want to explain to you what happened. Please hear me out."

She sighed and settled back on the couch. "Very well. What is it?"

He took a deep breath. "That night I lay awake for hours thinking how peaceful it was at home and how I was going back to what I thought was my certain death. I knew you were spending the night with Jessica, but I didn't expect to find you when I went into the kitchen in the wee hours. You were so kind and understanding of my feelings as we began to talk. And you were so beautiful. I wanted you to help me forget all the death I'd seen since I'd been gone. I never meant for it to go any further than talking."

"But then you kissed me."

He exhaled. "I did, and I liked it. That scared me more than anything."

She frowned. "Why?"

"I knew you'd had a crush on me ever since you and Jessica were kids, and I'd tried to tell myself you were like my kid sister. But that night I knew it wasn't true. You could be more to me, and I wasn't about to let that happen."

She frowned. "I don't understand."

"I'd written too many letters to the girlfriends and wives of my friends who were killed, and I didn't want anyone to have to send you a letter like that. I thought it was better if I cut our relationship off before it ever got started."

She sank back against the pillows of the couch and stared at him. "So you said those awful things to me about how we could never have a relationship because you wanted to protect me?"

"Yes."

She didn't say anything for a moment. Then she took a deep breath. "Thank you for telling me this, Adam. I've always thought it was because of me, that I wasn't good enough for you."

"No, Claire. It was all about me. That may seem self-ish to you now, but at the time it seemed the best course of action for me. I hope this will open up the possibility for us to be friends in the future. After all, you've always been like a part of our family."

"I would like for us to be friends, too, Adam."

He smiled. "Good. Then we'll start with your agreeing to something I'm going to propose."

"What?"

"I'm sorry we didn't know how tough things were for you after your father died, but you have to admit you did distance yourself from us."

"I know, and I'm sorry about that now."

He frowned at her. "You should be, but you can make it up to us."

"How?"

"The only case I'm working on right now is capturing James Lester. Since he is connected to Peter Willis, it just stands to reason that we work together to find them. What do you say?"

She arched an eyebrow. "Do you really want to work together or is this your way of trying to protect me from getting in over my head again?"

"Both. Jessica and I are worried that you don't have enough experience in this kind of work. It's to your advantage to join with me. It will be an opportunity for you to see what bounty hunting is all about, in case you decide you want to keep at it instead of going back to your boring librarian's job."

She laughed. "Boring? How do you know what my life is like?"

He shook his head. "I don't. But I'd like to make sure you can go back to it if you decide that's what you want. I don't want to see you get hurt. Please let me help you."

She took a deep breath and nodded. "Okay. I suppose that's the sensible thing to do. What do you suggest we do first?"

He glanced at his watch. "I'd say we need to get some sleep and talk about this over coffee in the morning."

She pushed to her feet and wobbled for a moment as she balanced herself. He stood and reached for her, but she pushed his hands away and shook her head. "No, I need to do this myself. If I'm going to become a bounty hunter, I can't let a little pain get to me."

She took a deep breath and took a step. Pain flickered across her face, and she bit down on her bottom lip. She took another step and then another. When she'd reached the guest bedroom door, she looked over her shoulder at him. "See? I'm better already."

He nodded, and she hobbled into the room and closed the door behind her. He yawned, went to the hall closet and pulled out the blanket and pillow Jessica stored there. He carried them back to the couch and settled down.

Adam had expected to drop off to sleep right away, but he couldn't. His mind raced with everything that had happened tonight. When he'd followed James Lester's trail to that cabin in Mississippi, he'd had no idea that it would lead to the almost fatal reunion with Claire and the realization that the bail jumper he was after was also involved in the murder of Claire's father.

Twice tonight she'd nearly been killed, and with James and Peter already facing murder charges they wouldn't hesitate to kill her the next time they met her. In fact, they were probably planning how they could get rid of her right now.

He pulled the blanket up to his chin. They could plan all they wanted to, but they were going to have to go through him first to get to her. He smiled. Those two killers were about to get an education in the meaning of his great-grandfather's words, which had inspired every bounty hunter at the Knight Agency for over a hundred years.

"James and Peter," he whispered. "We're coming for you. It's time for you to pay for the charges laid against you."

Claire sat up in bed, rubbed her eyes and inhaled the smell of coffee and the sweet aroma of something baking. She glanced at the bedside clock, and her eyes grew large—8:00 a.m. When had she ever slept that late? But then again when had she ever had a night like the one she'd just experienced?

She threw back the covers and swung her legs over the side of the bed. Tentatively, she pressed her feet to the floor before she took a deep breath and stood. A small pain in her ankle caused her to wince, but it wasn't as bad as it had been last night. She took a step and smiled. Either her injury had improved or she was managing to deal with it better.

Within minutes she was dressed. Now to walk into the kitchen and appear as though she'd made a full recovery. She took a deep breath and hobbled to the bedroom door. When she opened it, she could hear voices coming from the kitchen.

She made her way there and stopped at the door. Jessica and Adam sat at the kitchen table. Jessica looked up when Claire entered and smiled. "Hey, sleepyhead. I thought I was going to have to leave before you woke up."

"I'm glad you didn't. I wanted to thank you for everything you did for me last night."

Jessica pushed to her feet. "That's what friends are for. You would have done the same for me. Now sit down and let me get you some coffee and one of these apple Danish rolls. They're really good."

Claire inhaled a deep breath, and her stomach growled. "They smell delicious. I didn't get around to eating dinner last night, so I'm starved."

Adam took a sip from his cup and set it back in the saucer. "You'd better eat up this morning. We have a full day ahead of us."

Jessica set a cup of coffee and a plate with a Danish on it in front of Claire and glanced at her watch. "I have to get on the road. You two make yourselves at home." She turned to her brother. "I talked to the building superintendent this morning. He's going to repair the back door where James broke in, and he's going to put dead bolts on the front and back. I wish you would check and make sure it gets done."

Adam nodded. "I will. Be careful. And remember, don't let your guard down a minute with this guy you're bringing back. He'll try to make you think he's your friend, but he's not. He's a fugitive of the court."

Jessica rolled her eyes and smiled. "I know, big brother. I've done this before." She reached out and squeezed Claire's hand. "And you two be careful. I don't want anything to happen to either of you."

"We will be," Claire said. "And thanks again."

Jessica nodded, shrugged into her jacket and walked out the back door. When she was gone, a silence fell over the room. Claire picked up her cup and took a drink before she glanced back at Adam. The muscle in his jaw flexed as he stared into his coffee.

After a moment he glanced up. "How are you this morning?"

"I'm fine. A little sore, but I guess that's to be expected after last night."

He nodded. "But you seem to be walking better."

"It still hurts some, but I'm ready for the day. What should we do first?"

"We never got around to looking at Peter's cell phone last night. Maybe there's something on it that he didn't want us to see. Since James seemed to be interested in stealing the phone, I think we should look at it."

"I laid it on the dresser in the bedroom." Claire braced her arms on the table and started to push up.

Adam reached out and touched her arm. "Don't get up. I'll bring it in here."

Within minutes he was back at the table and scrolling through the contacts. When he didn't say anything, Claire leaned closer. "Spotted anything suspicious yet?"

He stopped and stared at the phone. "Here's something interesting. Numbers for three locations of a Serenity Wellness Spa."

Claire's eyes grew wide. "Did you say Serenity Wellness Spa?"

Adam glanced at her. "Yes. Have you heard of them before?"

"No. Not of the spas. But it's strange because before my father died, he was unconscious, but he kept mumbling. It sounded like he was saying the word *serene*, but I couldn't be sure. Maybe he was trying to tell me something. Where are these spas located?"

"One in Knoxville, one in Nashville and another near Memphis. They're in all of the major Tennessee cities."

"Do you think we should call one?"

Adam grinned at her. "I think we should. And you

deserve to make the call since you almost got killed trying to keep James from getting his hands on this phone."

She rolled her eyes at the teasing tone of his voice and punched in the number with the East Tennessee area code. It rang several times before a woman answered. "Thank you for calling the Smoky Mountain Serenity Wellness Spa. May I help you?"

Claire cleared her throat. "Yes. I just recently heard about your facility and wondered what you offer your guests."

"Serenity is basically a wellness resort that is designed to address the needs of the total individual. To do this we engage our guests in one-on-one stress-management techniques and promote physical involvement in activities such as hiking, massage, weight loss and workouts with a personal trainer. We strive to equip our guests with the tools necessary to face life in the twenty-first century."

"That sounds like what I'm looking for, but it may be too pricey for me," Claire said.

"Not necessarily. You can choose from different packages and tailor your program to fit your personal needs. All our options are available on our website. You might want to check them out and decide which sounds right for you. I can give you that address."

Claire wrote down the web address as the woman rattled it off. "Thank you for all your help. I'll be in touch if I decide to make a reservation."

"If I can be of any more help, please give me a call. I'll be glad to answer any of your questions. Goodbye."

Claire ended the call and shrugged. "It sounded like a really nice wellness spa. I'll call the one near Nashville and see what I find out there."

Ten minutes later she ended the call and sighed. "That conversation was almost a repeat of the earlier one. They must train their sales reps on exactly what to say."

"Are you going to call the one near here?"

"No. Why don't we drive out there and check it out?"

Adam drained his coffee cup, stood and put his dirty dishes in the dishwasher. "That sounds like a good idea. But before we do, I think we should talk to Peter's boss first. Have you been to see him yet?"

"I went by the bank a few days ago, but he wasn't in. One of the loan officers said he wouldn't be back until yesterday. So he should be in the office today."

"Then let's go get your car, and then we'll go pay a visit to the bank where Peter worked first. What's his boss's name?"

"Arthur Kendall is the bank's chief executive officer, but Whitney Hamilton is the chief financial officer." Claire glanced down at the smudges left on her shirt from when she fell to the ground the night before. "I'm still wearing the clothes I had on last night. Could we go by my house and let me wash some of this grime off before we take off for the day?"

"No problem. Are you ready to go now?"

Claire swallowed the last bite of Danish and washed it down with coffee before she stacked the dishes and rose. "I will be as soon as I put these in the dishwasher."

"Let me."

Adam reached for the dishes, and his fingers brushed against hers. Claire's pulse pounded, and she glanced down at the plate they both held. When she looked up, he was staring at her with an expression that left her breathless. He gave a tug on the dishes, and she loosened her grip.

"Thank you."

He smiled, and her heart raced. Her gaze swept over the room, and as it did she remembered another kitchen and a night when he'd looked at her in that way. What was she thinking? The excitement she'd been feeling a moment ago disappeared, and the bitterness she'd felt for years toward Adam resurfaced.

Last night they had agreed to try to be friends again, and she hoped they could be. But there was never going to be anything else between them. The dreams she'd once had about them were dead. Now all she wanted from him was help finding her father's killer. Nothing else.

FIVE

Adam glanced at Claire from time to time as he drove toward her father's house on the northern outskirts of Memphis. She'd been quiet ever since they left Jessica's apartment. He'd been pleased with how well their conversation had gone until suddenly she clammed up and had barely spoken since.

He turned onto the gravel path that led to the farmhouse Claire's father had purchased a few years ago and stopped behind a truck in the driveway. "Whose truck?"

"It belonged to my father. I've been trying to sell it, but so far no one has been interested." She opened the door, climbed out and headed to the front door. "Come on inside. You can wait in the living room while I'm getting cleaned up."

He followed her into the house and glanced around the neat room they'd entered. The leather furniture and the sports magazines on the coffee table reminded him of Claire's dad. He sat down on the couch and picked up one of the magazines.

"Take your time. I'll entertain myself."

She nodded and disappeared down a hallway, which he assumed led to the bedrooms. He thumbed through the magazine and read several articles before he tossed it back on the coffee table and chose another one.

Thirty minutes later he glanced up as Claire walked back into the room. She'd changed into jeans and a red sweater that seemed to bring out the highlights in her chestnut-colored hair. For a moment all he could do was stare at her. Then he laid the magazine down and rose.

She smiled. "I hope you didn't get bored while I was gone."

He shook his head. "I read several of your dad's magazines." He glanced around the room and noticed for the first time the family pictures sitting on tables and a large painting of Claire and her mother hanging on the wall. He walked over and gazed up at the painting. "Your mother was a very beautiful woman."

"Yes, she was," Claire murmured.

He turned and faced her. "With you away in Nashville after your mother passed away, your father must have wanted to be surrounded by his memories."

"He did." She hesitated before continuing. "I should have come home more often, but I told myself I was busy. If I'd known our time would be short, I would have come more often."

"Don't blame yourself. I think that's human nature to become so involved in what you're doing that you let some things slide. I know I don't visit my parents like I should, and they live right here in Memphis."

"Why don't you visit them?"

He shrugged. "I don't know. It just seems like every time I go over there, they try to get me to go to church with them. They know I'm not into that kind of stuff."

Claire's eyebrows arched. "'That kind of stuff'? There's nothing more important than your relationship with God. They keep reminding you of that because they love you, and they want you to realize how much God loves you."

"God?" he sneered. "Where was God when my buddies were being blown to bits right before my eyes in battle? He should have showed up if He loves us so much."

A somber expression covered her face. "He showed up for you, didn't He? You came home."

He raked his hand through his hair. "I don't want to talk about this now. We need to go get your car and get it back here so we can go to the bank this afternoon and talk to Peter's boss before we go to the spa."

"All right. I'm ready."

Adam strode from the house to his car. When Claire climbed into the passenger seat, he gunned the motor, and they roared out of the driveway and headed back into the city. He glanced at her from time to time, but she stared straight ahead without speaking.

After a few miles, he took a deep breath. "I'm sorry that I spoke to you the way I did. It's just that I hear all that talk about God from my folks and Jessica all the time. I didn't expect to hear it from you, too."

She turned her head and stared at him. "I thought you knew that my faith has always been important to me. I don't know how I would have survived after my father's death if I hadn't had it."

"I respect that. It's important to you, but it's not for me. Can we just leave it at that?"

She smiled, but her face held a hint of sadness. "If that's the way you want it."

"It is," he said and directed his gaze back to the highway.

She reached over and tuned the radio to the station

she'd listened to last night on the way back from Mississippi. The music of a Christian rock band filled the car. He gritted his teeth and didn't say anything.

An hour and a half later they arrived at the road that led to Peter's cabin, and Claire directed him to the spot where she'd parked her car the night before. Her heart sank when she spotted the vehicle.

Adam stopped behind it, and they both got out to inspect it. The windows and windshield were shattered, and all four tires were pierced with bullet holes. Claire propped her hands on her hips and sighed. "It looks like they took out their anger on my poor car."

Adam squatted beside one of tires and ran his finger over the surface. "They probably did this when they fired at us in the cabin. If I'd checked before I left to take you to the hospital, we could have contacted someone this morning to haul your car back to Memphis."

"Do you know a company that could transport it for me?"

Adam rose to his feet and brushed his hands together. "I have some friends that I can call. They should be able to get the car back to Memphis. I'm not sure if it can be repaired though. There are bullet holes in all the doors and the hood."

She nodded. "I suppose they wanted to send me a message in case they hadn't killed us. They probably wanted me to know they hadn't given up."

"Don't think like that, Claire. These guys aren't going to get to you. I'll see to that."

"I should have known better than to think I could stand up against Peter Willis. He's killed at least once, and he was ready to do it again last night. If it hadn't been for you and Jessica, I'd be dead now."

"But you're not. And I'm going to see that nothing happens to you."

She shook her head. "I've already put you and Jessica in enough danger. I don't want you risking your life to take care of me."

He grinned. "You don't have anything to say in the matter. We're going after Willis and Lester, and we're going to make them pay for what they've done." He pulled his cell phone from his pocket. "Now I'm going to call the wrecker service and tell them where to find the car. Then we're going to Arthur Kendall's office."

Claire let her gaze travel over the car again and back to him. "Thanks, Adam. After everything that's happened in the past twenty-four hours, I know I really should have come to you in the first place instead of trying to do it on my own."

Her words surprised him. As long as he'd known her, she'd been independent and would hesitate before accepting help for anything. But she seemed to understand she'd crossed a dangerous line last night, one she wished she hadn't.

He watched her climb back into his car, and a strong desire to protect her overcame him. He'd tried to tell himself he was helping her because his sister asked him to do it, but he knew that wasn't true. He was doing it for himself.

No matter what he'd said to her years ago at his parents' home, he'd never been able to forget how beautiful she'd looked that night and how he'd felt when he kissed her. It did him no good, however, to dwell on that night because there was no going back and undoing the damage his hateful words had caused. If he could keep her safe and help her find the man who'd killed her father, maybe he'd be on the path to gaining her forgiveness. Then the only problem would be figuring out how he could ever forgive himself for destroying something that could have been the best thing that ever happened to him.

Claire glanced around the bank where Peter had worked as they stepped inside. Tellers busied themselves with customers and didn't look up when they headed to the elevators that led to the upper floors where the bank's offices were located.

The elevator doors opened as they approached, and a bank employee who had been waiting stepped inside. He held the door for them to get on and smiled. "Which floor?" he asked.

"Three," Claire replied.

"Me, too," he said. He stared at Claire for a moment. "I think I've seen you before. Are you a bank customer?"

She shook her head. "No, I was in last week to see Mr. Kendall, and he wasn't here. I hope he is today."

The man nodded. "He is. In fact, I'm on my way to his office to take him some papers. I'll be glad to direct you there."

Claire smiled. "Thanks. What is your position here at the bank?"

"I'm a loan officer."

She glanced at Adam and then back to the man. "Then I suppose you knew Peter Willis when he worked here."

The smile on his face disappeared, and he cleared his throat. "We worked on different accounts, so I didn't see him all that often. But I did know him." He frowned and studied Claire for a moment. "If you aren't a bank customer, how did you know Peter Willis worked here?"

"My father's bail bond company posted his bail. Now he's disappeared, and we're out the money we paid the court."

The man's eyebrows arched. "Oh, I see. Then I suppose you'd like to recover your money."

"I would, but I have to find him first."

The elevator stopped on the third floor, and they got off. The man pointed down the hallway. "Mr. Kendall's office is the second door on the right."

Adam stepped up beside him. "I thought you said you were going to his office, too."

"I was. I mean I am, but I need to take care of a matter in Mr. Hamilton's office first."

He turned and hurried down the hall in the opposite direction from them. Claire and Adam stared at his retreating figure, then turned to each other. "He seemed to be in a hurry to get away," Adam said.

"Yeah. The mention of Peter Willis seemed to upset him." She shrugged and turned toward the office. "Let's go see if Arthur Kendall is any more talkative."

They stopped outside the office the man had pointed out and pushed the door open. A receptionist looked up from a computer and smiled when they entered the office. "Come in. May I help you?"

Claire had to control herself to keep from rolling her eyes when Adam returned the woman's smile with the one he always used when he was trying to get someone to do something for him. "We don't have an appointment, but we'd like to speak with Mr. Kendall if it's possible."

"If it's about a loan, we have employees who can help you with that."

Adam shook his head. "No, it's about one of his employees."

The woman darted a glance at Claire then back at Adam. "Which one?"

"Peter Willis."

The woman's eyes grew large. "Are you with the police?"

"No," Adam replied. "We're bounty hunters who are trying to find Willis and bring him back to jail."

"Mr. Willis is no longer an employee here, and Mr. Kendall is in a meeting with our chief financial officer right now, but I'll see if he has time to talk with you." She picked up her telephone and punched a number. "Mr. Kendall, there are two people here who would like to talk to you about Peter Willis." She paused for a moment before she spoke again. "No, sir. They're bounty hunters."

Before she could replace the phone in its cradle, the inner office door opened, and a man strode through the door. His gaze swept Claire and then Adam. He stuck out his hand and shook her hand, then his. "I'm Arthur Kendall. Miss Hopkins tells me you want to talk to me about Peter Willis."

Adam nodded. "Yes. I'm Adam Knight of the Knight Fugitive Recovery Agency, and this is Claire Walker, the owner of Walker's Bail Bonds. We won't take much of your time."

He motioned toward his office. "Come in. Would you like something to drink while we're talking? Coffee? A soft drink?"

"No, thank you," Claire replied.

As they entered the office, a man who'd been sitting

at a small conference table at the side of the room rose and smiled. Mr. Kendall pointed to him. "This is Whitney Hamilton. We were just finishing up a meeting," Mr. Kendall continued.

Adam stopped and turned to Mr. Kendall. "We didn't mean to disturb you. We can come back later if that would be more convenient for you."

Whitney Hamilton shook his head and began to gather up the papers on the desk. "It's no problem. We're already through." He stuck the papers in a folder and moved his chair back up to the table. "Mr. Kendall said you're bounty hunters, and you're after Peter Willis."

Adam nodded. "Actually, I'm a bounty hunter, and Miss Walker owns the bail bond company that paid Willis's bail. She would like to see him caught so she won't lose the money she put up for his bail."

He looked at Claire and shook his head. "I'm so sorry, Miss Walker. I hope you find him soon. If I can do anything, let me know. Now I'll get back to my office and leave you with Mr. Kendall."

Before the man could leave, Adam spoke. "Did you work with Peter?"

"I did. I oversee all the financial operations of the bank, and he was one of our loan officers. We were all shocked when he was arrested."

"We may need to ask you some questions later about the loans that Peter approved."

Mr. Hamilton darted a glance at Arthur Kendall. "I'm afraid I don't have the authority to do that on my own, but anything Mr. Kendall tells me to do, I will. Good day and good luck with your search."

He walked toward the door but stopped when he got

there. "I'll catch you later, Arthur, about that decision we need to make."

Arthur Kendall nodded. "I'll call you when I get a chance."

Mr. Kendall walked over and closed the door behind his employee and motioned for Adam and Claire to sit in the two chairs facing his desk. He walked around to his desk chair and eased into it before he rested his arms in front of him on his desk, laced his fingers together and stared at Adam. "So you're Adam Knight. I've heard of your agency, Mr. Knight. Your bounty hunter organization has been around a long time in Memphis."

"Yes, it has."

Mr. Kendall frowned. "And how can I help you today?"

Claire spoke up. "Were you aware that Peter jumped bail?"

Mr. Kendall's eyebrows arched. "Yes, but I only found out recently. I couldn't believe it when he was accused of killing one of our employees. I was sure the police had made a mistake and vouched for his integrity and ties to the community in helping him get bail. I can't believe I was so deceived."

"I'm sorry," Claire said. "My father posted the bail, and when he tried to apprehend Peter, he was killed."

"Are you saying that Peter killed your father?"

Claire nodded. "I am. Since he's jumped bail, it looks more incriminating for him on the first charge against him."

Mr. Kendall leaned back in his chair and stared at her in disbelief. "The Peter I knew was a good bank employee and wasn't someone you'd ever suspect of murder. That's why I thought the police had made a mistake in accusing him of Lance Morgan's murder. The evidence they had was all circumstantial."

Adam leaned forward in his chair. "They must have had something or they wouldn't have accused him."

"Maybe so," Mr. Kendall said. "I just thought they jumped to conclusions before they should have."

"What did Lance Morgan do here at the bank?" Claire asked.

"He was a loan officer, too. He worked with Peter on some of his loans, and I thought Lance would have a great future here. Then the police found him dead in his car in the driveway of his home. I thought it was a robbery gone bad, but the police disagreed."

Claire took a deep breath. "Well, you haven't seen the side of Peter that I saw last night when he told me he killed my father."

Mr. Kendall directed an angry glare in her direction. "You shouldn't make accusations like that, Miss Walker. Not unless you have proof."

"Oh, I have firsthand proof all right. He told me he did it right before he tried to kill me."

"He tried to kill you?" A look of disbelief flashed across the man's face.

"Yes. In fact, he tried to kill both of us."

"The things you're saying don't sound like the Peter I know. He's always been an upstanding citizen and a good family man."

Adam leaned forward in his chair. "It sounds like you didn't know him as well as you thought you did. Have you had any contact with Peter since he was arrested?"

He shook his head. "He came into the office when he made bail, and I told him we were putting him on temporary leave until his legal problems were cleared up. I haven't seen him since."

"What about his friend James Lester?"

Mr. Kendall frowned and shook his head. "I've never heard that name. You say he's a friend of Peter's?"

"Yes," Claire said. "He was with Peter when he tried to kill us, and then Lester broke into the apartment where I was staying last night."

"Do the police know all this?" Mr. Kendall asked.

"They do. They're looking for both of them, too. We just need to know if there's anything you can tell us that could help us track down Peter."

Mr. Kendall shook his head. "My relationship with Peter was strictly professional. We didn't socialize outside of work except for bank functions. His wife attended all our dinners and parties with him, and he appeared devoted to her."

"What kind of employee was he?" Adam asked.

"He was a good loan officer. He was diligent in his work, and I had no problems with him at all."

"I see," Adam said. "What types of loans did he handle for the bank?"

Mr. Kendall shrugged. "He worked with all types, but he mainly dealt with commercial loans."

"Commercial, huh?" Adam glanced at Claire. "Did he have a connection to a company named Serenity that has three wellness spas in the state?"

Mr. Kendall hesitated a moment before he answered. "I'm afraid I can't answer that."

"Why?"

He sighed. "Mr. Knight, I'm willing to give you any help I can in finding Peter, but I can't discuss private bank matters with you."

The two men stared at each other as if daring the other to blink. Finally Adam's mouth curled into a half smile. "Your answer leads me to suspect that Serenity does business with your bank."

Mr. Kendall shook his head. "It wouldn't matter what I said. If I denied it, you would assume I was lying. If I confirmed it, I would be violating the ethics of this institution. Since you're not with the police and don't have a search warrant, my best option is to remain silent. If the police want to look at our records, they can get a warrant. I'll be happy to cooperate with them any way I can."

Claire glanced at Adam, and he stood and handed his card to Mr. Kendall. "If you won't answer our questions, then I assume it won't do any good to talk to Mr. Hamilton."

"No, I'm afraid not."

"We appreciate the time you've given us today. If you think of anything about Peter that you can tell us, give me a call."

"I'll be glad to do that, Mr. Knight. Good day."

Adam and Claire murmured their goodbyes and headed toward the door. When they stepped into the hallway outside the office, Claire spotted the young man who'd shown them to Mr. Kendall's office earlier. He stood beside the elevator.

As they approached, he took a step toward them and brushed past Claire. "Meet me in the parking lot," he whispered before he disappeared into the stairwell that led to the exit.

Claire glanced up at Adam. "Did you hear that?"

His grim face told her the answer even before he spoke. "Yes."

He grabbed her by the elbow and led her into the elevator when the doors opened. Neither spoke as they descended to the first floor of the building.

They hurried through the lobby and exited the building. Once outside, Claire turned to Adam. "What do you think he wants?"

"I don't know, but the way he acted, he doesn't want anyone to overhear him."

Claire scanned the parking lot as they headed to their car. They'd almost reached it when they heard a voice whisper, "I'm over here."

The young man stood at the back corner of the bank building. Claire's heart raced as they walked toward him. Did he have some information that could help them find Peter? Or was he connected to Peter Willis and James Lester?

She swallowed the panic rising in her throat and glanced at Adam beside her.

He didn't take his eyes off the figure standing beside the building. Then slowly he unbuttoned his jacket and let it hang open. She glanced down and caught a glimpse of the gun holstered at his waist, and her heart beat even faster. Adam was ready for whatever might occur.

SIX

Adam's eyes narrowed as he studied the man they'd first seen inside the bank. He still seemed as jumpy as he had when they'd gotten off the elevator together. As Adam and Claire approached, he kept looking over his shoulder as if he expected someone to come out the back door of the bank at any minute.

They stopped in front of him, and Adam stared into his eyes. "You wanted to speak with us?"

He nodded, and a drop of perspiration trickled down the side of his face. "I didn't want anyone inside to see me talking to you. That's why I asked you to meet me here."

"Who are you?" Adam asked.

"My name is Jonathan Fields. I've worked as a loan officer at this bank for five years now."

"And you said you knew Peter Willis?"

Jonathan glanced over his shoulder again before he stepped closer. "Look, I don't want to cause any trouble for the bank. I like my job here, and Mr. Kendall has been very good to me. But I always thought there was something strange about Willis."

"Like what?"

"He was supposed to be a loan officer, but he acted more like a public-relations person. He was always representing the bank at community functions such as golf tournaments or business openings. He didn't keep the same hours that the rest of us did and wasn't in the office much. The rumor was that he had family connections inside the bank, and he could pretty much do as he chose."

"But his job was to work with loans, wasn't it?"

"That's what his job title was, but as far as I could tell, he only had one client. But it was the largest one the bank had, a company named Serenity Wellness Centers. They have three spas across the state, some in Arkansas, and a few in Georgia."

"That's interesting," Adam said. He let the conversation in Arthur Kendall's office run through his mind again before he spoke. "What about Lance Morgan? Did you know him?"

"I did. He was a good guy. Married to his high school sweetheart. As I understand it, Mr. Kendall has been very kind to her and has helped her a lot since her husband's death."

"Did you ever suspect there was any trouble between Peter and Lance?"

Jonathan shook his head. "Not when they first began working together. But the day Lance was killed I had overheard him having an argument with Peter."

Adam inched closer. "What did they say?"

Jonathan glanced over his shoulder once more before lowering his voice. "I went to the break room to get a cup of coffee, but there was none left. I went into the storage room that's behind the break area to get a new package of coffee, and I had just started to go back when the break room door slammed. Then I heard angry voices.

I didn't want to get in the middle of an argument, so I eased the storage room door until it was almost closed. But I could still hear what was being said."

"Was it Peter and Lance?" Claire asked.

"Yes. At first Peter was yelling at Lance saying he didn't have anything on him and that he couldn't prove anything. Then Lance said, 'I've suspected things weren't right for a long time. You've been lucky so far, but it won't be long before the auditors catch on to you.'"

"Something was wrong with Peter's books?" Adam asked.

"So Lance seemed to think. Peter told him he didn't know what he was talking about, and that the auditors wouldn't find anything because there was nothing to find. Then Lance said, 'We'll see what Mr. Kendall has to say when I go to him with my suspicions.'"

"How did Peter react to that?"

"I heard what sounded like a struggle, and I peeked through the door crack to see what was going on. Peter had his hands around Lance's neck and had him pushed up against the wall. He got right down in his face and muttered, 'You go to Mr. Kendall, and it'll be the last thing you'll ever do.' That night Lance was killed when he stopped his car in the driveway at his home."

Adam heard Claire suck in her breath, and he glanced around at her. "Have you told anybody else what you heard?" she asked.

"The next day when I heard Lance had been killed, I went to the police and told them what I'd heard. A few days later they came to the bank and arrested Peter on suspicion of murder. He hired a lawyer and was out of jail in no time. Now you say he's jumped bail."

Adam cocked his head to one side and studied Jonathan. "Why are you telling us all this?"

Jonathan's lips quivered and Adam could see fear in his eyes. "Because I'm scared. I'm convinced Peter killed Lance because he was about to go to Mr. Kendall. I don't know what it was, but I'm sure it got Lance killed. Now that I know he's jumped bail, I'm afraid he'll come after me if he finds out I've talked to the police. I want to help you find him."

Adam nodded. "I hope we can." He pulled out his card and handed it to Jonathan. "Call me if you think of anything else or if you see Peter."

Jonathan took the card and stuck it in his pocket. "I will, and I hope you catch him soon. I'll sleep a lot better when he's back in jail."

He turned to leave, but Adam called out to him. "One more thing."

Jonathan turned back toward them. "What?"

"Do you know James Lester?"

He pursed his lips and thought for a moment before he shook his head. "I don't think I've ever heard that name. Sorry."

"That's okay. Take care of yourself."

Jonathan nodded. "I will."

Adam and Claire watched as he turned and hurried back into the bank. When he had disappeared inside, Adam faced Claire. "I think we need to visit the Serenity Wellness Center."

"Do you want to go now?"

Adam looked at his watch. "It's almost lunchtime. Why don't we grab a bite to eat and go out there this afternoon?"

Claire shrugged. "Sounds good to me. Where do you want to go?"

"There's a new place down the street from our office. Since it's on the way to Serenity, we can eat there."

"All right."

She turned and walked toward the car. He watched her for a moment before he followed. She'd been quiet ever since they'd left her house earlier this morning. It had to be hard for her being back in her father's house and surrounded by all the pictures of the people she'd loved.

As she strode across the parking lot, he noticed how straight her back was and how she had her fists clenched at her side. His heart pricked at the thought that with her father gone, she was really alone in the world. He couldn't imagine how that must feel. He still had his parents and his brother and sister. Now she had no one.

But that really wasn't true. She might not realize it, but she still had friends. She had Jessica, and although she might not want to admit it, she had him. And he would do anything he could to help during this painful time.

The thought had no sooner flashed in his mind than he heard the roar of a car engine. He looked toward the back of the bank, and a black car with tinted windows careened around the corner of the building. The driver didn't slow but accelerated the car. As it barreled forward, Adam realized that Claire had just stepped into a lane between two rows of cars, and the car was headed straight for her.

"Claire!" he yelled at the top of his voice. "Watch out!"

She stopped and stared at the approaching car but seemed frozen in place. "Claire!" he yelled again.

She didn't move.

Without taking time to think, Adam lunged forward. He grabbed Claire and wrapped his arms around her waist. Before he could get them clear of the vehicle's path, he felt the impact of the car against his leg. His last conscious thought was that he hadn't been quick enough.

Claire lay on the ground with her body wedged under the bumper of Adam's car. For a moment she couldn't remember what had happened. Then it all rushed back into her mind. A speeding car. Adam shouting her name. And then the sensation of being thrown across the parking lot.

She tried to move but couldn't. Something held her down.

She turned her head to peer over her shoulder and gasped. Adam lay on top of her. Blood trickled from a cut on his forehead, and his eyes were closed.

Fear welled up in her. Was he alive? If he had been killed trying to protect her, how could she ever forgive herself? And how could she face Jessica and the Knight family?

She took a deep breath. "Adam!" she screamed. "Please wake up!"

When he didn't move, she tried to wriggle free, but it was no use. She couldn't move his still form. She lay motionless for another moment and then pushed against him again. Still no movement.

Then she heard a man's voice. "Miss, are you all right?"

She turned her head so that she could barely see past Adam's body. All she could make out was a pair of tennis shoes. "Don't move. I've called 911," the man said. "Just lie still until they get here. I don't want to pull your friend free and take a chance on injuring him."

"I-is h-he br-breathing?" She could barely make herself voice the question.

"He is," the man answered. "Don't worry about him. The paramedics will be here in no time, and they will take care of both of you."

"Thank you." She lay still for a moment. "Who are you?"

"My name is Jordan. I'm a student at the University of Memphis, and I was on my way to the bank when I saw a car hit the two of you."

"Did the driver stop?"

"No," Jordan said. "It just kept going. Your friend was mighty brave the way he charged across the parking lot and protected you."

Another tear trickled down her face. "Yes, he is quite brave. I owe him my life. I hope it hasn't cost him his."

"I don't think…" But his words were cut short by the squeal of tires and the blare of sirens. "The paramedics are here—and the police. I'll get out of the way and let them do their job."

She heard running footsteps and then a voice. "We're EMTs, and we're going to get you out of here, miss. But first we need to check this man before we move him."

"Yes, please see if you can help him. I think I'm all right."

Within minutes the EMTs had done a quick check of Adam and lifted him off her. Then they reached down and gently pulled her out from under the car's bumper. When she was free, she tried to sit up, but everything around her appeared to be moving.

"Take it easy," one of the EMTs said. "Let me check you over."

A few minutes later he'd completed his initial examination. "Everything looks good so far. You're very lucky. From what I can tell your friend's body cushioned you from the blow of the car's impact."

Guilt filled her heart, and she wished she could take back all the hateful things she'd said or thought about Adam in the past few years. He had promised her he would protect her, and he had done that. She hoped she would have the chance to thank him.

A gurney sat next to the ambulance with its back doors open, and she could see Adam lying on it. A uniformed police officer stood beside him while he wrote something on a notepad. "Adam? Is he okay?" she asked.

The EMT helped her into a sitting position, completed his check for broken bones and smiled at her. "I'm sure they'll let us know how he is in a moment, but I need to make sure you're not injured."

She shook her head. "Really I'm fine. I need to go check on him, though."

Claire tried to push to her feet, but the EMT put a restraining hand on her shoulder. "Wait a minute. I'll go check on your friend for you."

He was gone for few minutes before he returned. "How is he?" she asked.

The EMT grinned. "He's awake and insisting he needs to get back to work. My partner thinks he needs to get checked out at the hospital, but he says he doesn't want to go."

"Let me talk to him. Maybe I can convince him to go."

The man helped Claire to her feet, and she held on to his arm and waited for the dizziness to pass before she walked toward the gurney. Adam looked up at her and smiled when she stopped beside him.

"Are you okay?"

She nodded. "I am, thanks to you. What's this I'm hearing about you refusing to go to the hospital?"

He sat up and swung his legs over the side of the gurney. "I'm okay. I had worse happen to me in combat."

"But this is different. You may have internal injuries that you aren't aware of."

He rubbed the back of his neck and frowned. "Look, Claire, we need to get after these guys. I can't do that if I'm laid up in a hospital."

"But, Adam, I'm only thinking of what's best for you."

"Then let me decide what I need to do. Okay?"

She hesitated a moment, but the look in his eyes told her she was going to get nowhere in convincing him to go to the hospital. She exhaled a deep breath. "Okay, but on one condition. You let me take you to your parents' home and you stay there tonight so your mom can keep an eye on you. We can get back to work tomorrow."

He shook his head. "I won't agree to that."

She stepped closer to him, clenched her fists at her sides and frowned. "Yes you will if you know what's good for you. I've seen your mother angry and she'll be furious with you if I tell her what's happened, and that you are refusing any kind of help."

He looked at her for a moment, and then he grinned. "Yes, ma'am. I'd forgotten how ferocious you can be when somebody crosses you. I'll go to my parents' house."

She breathed a sigh of relief. "Good."

One of the EMTs stepped up as Adam climbed down from the gurney. "Where do you think you're going?"

Adam stumbled a bit when his feet hit the ground, and

Claire reached out and grabbed his arm. "Mr. Knight really doesn't want to go to the hospital. I'll take him home and have his mother watch him tonight. If she sees any problems, she'll have him to the ER in no time."

Adam's face flushed at the amused look that spread across the paramedic's face. "His mother, huh?"

Claire nodded. "She's a nurse. So I'm sure she's qualified."

The man sighed. "Okay, if that's the way he wants it. There don't seem to be any life-threatening injuries, but take it easy tonight."

"I will," Adam said. "And thank you."

The policeman spoke up before they could walk away. "Mr. Knight has told me all he can remember, but I need to get your story, too."

Claire shook her head. "I don't remember anything except seeing this black car bearing down on me and then Adam pushing me out of the way. When I woke up, the car was gone."

The policeman pursed his lips and nodded. "That's about all Mr. Knight remembers. Lucky for you that college student was in the parking lot. He got the license plate number. They're running it for me now."

A dispatcher's voice crackled on the officer's lapel mic. "10-43."

He pulled the mic closer to his mouth. "Go ahead."

A woman's voice spoke from the mic. "The car is registered to James Lester. At present there are arrest warrants on him for aggravated assault and fleeing custody."

"10-4." The policeman looked at Adam. "Do you know a James Lester?"

For the next few minutes Adam filled the officer in on the events of the past few days.

When he'd finished, the policeman completed the comments he had written in his notepad and nodded. "Okay. We'll stay in touch and let you know if we find him."

"Thanks," Adam said as he turned to Claire. "Now let's get out of here."

"I'm ready," she said and took him by the arm.

Together they walked to the car, and Claire opened the passenger door for him. She was just about to close it when Arthur Kendall and Whitney Hamilton ran into the parking lot toward their car. They skidded to a stop next to Claire. "Someone just came into my office and told me what happened out here. Are you two all right?" Whitney asked.

Claire closed the car door and smiled at them. "Thanks for checking on us but we are going to be fine."

Mr. Kendall glanced around at the gathered bystanders. "With this many people in the parking lot, surely someone was able to get a description of the car."

Claire pointed to the college student who was talking with the police officer. "That young man was on his way into the bank and saw the whole thing. He not only got a description of the car but also the license number."

Arthur Kendall breathed a sigh of relief. "Good for him. Maybe the police can catch whoever did this. Our bank has had enough bad publicity without two people being run down in our parking lot. I'm so relieved that both of you are okay. If there's an ambulance bill, tell the hospital that our insurance will cover it since the accident happened on our property."

"Thank you."

Claire walked around the car and climbed in behind

the steering wheel. Adam glanced at her. "What did they want?"

"They wanted to make sure we were okay and said that the bank's insurance would cover the cost of the ambulance since the accident happened on their property."

Adam's eyebrows arched. "Accident? That was no accident. It was deliberate attempt to kill both of us."

"I know."

Claire turned the ignition and glanced at Arthur Kendall and Whitney Hamilton, who were talking with police officers, before she pulled out into the afternoon traffic. Twenty minutes later she pulled into the East Memphis home of Adam's parents. She turned off the ignition and swiveled in the seat to face Adam. "Do you need me to help you into the house?"

"No, like you always say, I can do it on my own."

She grinned. "Yeah, I guess I do. In that case I'll take your car if you don't mind and return for you in the morning."

His eyes grew wide. "And just where do you think you're going?"

"Home."

He shook his head. "Oh, no, you're not. That car that almost ran us down was the same one that chased us into Memphis last night, and I'd say that it was either James or Peter driving it. So you're still not safe, and I'm not going to let you stay by yourself tonight."

She chuckled. "So where do you suggest I stay?"

He pointed to the house. "Right here. You practically grew up in Jessica's room, and it is just like she left it. You can stay there. Then in the morning we can start out again. What do you say?"

She thought about the farmhouse where her father

had lived and how isolated it was and then glanced back at the Knight's two-story brick house on a dead end street in a safe neighborhood. The choice should be a no-brainer. She'd always felt as if Adam's parents were her second mom and dad, and they would be happy to have her stay overnight again.

However, here was one big problem. Adam would be there with her in the same house where they'd been six years ago when he'd kissed her and then turned his back on her. Could she put those memories out of her mind?

She took a deep breath and squared her shoulders. Tomorrow Jessica would be back, and she could stay with her if need be. Tonight she didn't have a choice. She would be safer here.

Safer?

Maybe from James and Peter, but not from the man who still had the ability to make her heart race when he looked at her. She shook her head and followed Adam to the front door. All she had to do was stay away from him while they were here, and she'd be fine.

SEVEN

Adam sat up in bed and swung his feet to the floor—3:00 a.m. glowed on the bedside clock. He sat still for a moment in case the dizziness he'd felt earlier returned. When nothing happened, he climbed from bed and pulled on his jeans and a sweatshirt. He glanced around his childhood bedroom and smiled. He didn't come home often enough, he realized, but when he did it really made him feel good.

He walked to the bedroom door, stepped into the hall and listened for sounds in the house. The door to his parents' room was closed as was the one to the bedroom his brother had lived in before moving out. He stopped beside the closed door of the room where Claire was sleeping and paused. No sounds came from inside. As tired as she had been, she was probably dead to the world.

As quietly as possible, he moved down the staircase to the entry. As he walked down the hallway that led to the kitchen, he noticed the glow of a light coming from that direction. He chuckled at the thought that his mother had learned years ago that with two growing boys in the house she needed to leave a light on in case they needed a midnight snack.

He stopped at the kitchen door and flipped on the overhead light. A surprised squeal followed by a clatter split the nighttime quiet. Instinct kicked in, and he grabbed at the waist of his jeans for his gun. But it wasn't there.

Before he could say anything, Claire's angry voice rang out. "What do you mean, scaring me like that?"

For a moment he couldn't speak but could only take in the scene before him. Claire sat at the kitchen table, the cup she'd been drinking from overturned, and cocoa pooling on his mother's kitchen table.

He took a deep breath to calm his pounding heart and frowned. "Scaring you? If I'd had my gun with me, I would have shot you. You're supposed to be asleep."

Claire tilted her head to one side and crossed her arms. "So are you. I guess Peter and James aren't the only ones I have to worry about as far as my safety is concerned."

He couldn't help but smile. She might be grown-up, but she was still the saucy little girl who had always stood her ground with him. He glanced down at the mess in front of her, set the cup back in its saucer and reached for a paper towel. "Let me clean this up for you."

To his surprise she didn't argue but let him wipe up the spill. When he'd finished, she smiled. "Thanks, Adam. I'm sorry if I frightened you. I couldn't sleep and thought I'd make myself some cocoa."

"That sounds good. What if I make us both a cup?"

Her forehead wrinkled, and for a moment he thought she was going to refuse. Then she shrugged. "Sure. That sounds good."

A few minutes later they sat facing each other at the kitchen table as they quietly sipped from their cups.

Adam raised his cup to his lips and stared at Claire over the rim. A feeling of déjà vu hit him, and he almost choked.

Claire didn't appear to notice, and after a moment he set the cup back in its saucer. "Claire, I hope you're not uncomfortable being here with me."

She paused before she answered. "It does bring up memories of another night."

"I know. I've tried to explain what was going on with me at that time, but I'm sure it's not easy to understand." He sat still as the memories of seeing his buddies killed by roadside bombs and snipers rushed into his head. He closed his eyes and pressed his fingers against them. "I was so scared the whole time I was home. I didn't want to go back. I was sure I would never make it home again. Then I found you here, and for the first time I felt like I had someone I could talk to, but I was afraid of that, too. I knew it would be hard enough for my family if I didn't make it through the war, and I didn't want to add you to the list."

"I wish I had realized," she murmured.

He took a deep breath. "It's okay. If you haven't experienced combat, you can't begin to understand what it does to you." He pushed his cup away and stood. "Anyway, I don't want to think about that tonight. I want it to stay in the past where it belongs. Now I'd better get back to bed and leave you alone. I'll see you in the morning."

She reached out and grabbed his arm before he could walk away from the table. "Wait a minute. I want to say something to you."

"What?"

She swallowed and clenched her hands in her lap. "I wanted to thank you for saving my life at the bank. For some reason, I couldn't move. If you hadn't thrown me out of the way, I'd probably be dead. I'm so sorry that you ended up hurt."

He smiled. "Aw, don't worry about me. I'm okay. Besides, I promised you I'd protect you, and I wanted to do that."

She nodded. "I know. But when I woke up, I was wedged under the car, and I couldn't move you off me. I thought you were dead, and I was afraid I'd never have the chance to thank you and to apologize."

He frowned. "Apologize for what?"

She took a deep breath. "For holding a grudge against you all these years. I should have asked God to help me forgive you, but I didn't. Instead I concentrated on how rejected I'd felt that night you kissed me, and I let my anger against you fester into something ugly."

He sat back down at the table and reached his hand across the table. She hesitated a moment before she raised her hand from her lap and laced her fingers with his. Her touch sent a warm rush through him. "I was out of line that night, and there hasn't been a day since that I haven't regretted what I said. I think I ruined something that could have been good for both of us."

"Maybe so," she said. "But that's all in the past now. I want you to know that I have let it all go. I promise you that from now on I'll treasure your friendship, and I'll try to be a good friend to you, too."

He smiled, and his fingers tightened around hers. "That sounds good to me, Claire. Thank you for telling me." He squeezed her hand once more before he stood again. "Why don't you go on to bed? I'll clean up here, and Mom will never suspect her kitchen had visitors in the middle of the night."

She smiled and stood. "Okay. I'll see you in the morning."

"Sleep well."

He watched her go before he picked up the cups and carried them to the sink. He set them down, grabbed the edge of the counter and closed his eyes. At least she had forgiven him, but all she wanted was to be friends.

After the way he'd talked to her six years ago, he was lucky to have that much from her. Now all he needed to do was find a way to quit thinking about her every moment they were apart. That wasn't going to be easy.

To Claire's surprise, her lack of sleep the night before hadn't affected her as badly as she'd expected. Maybe it was the fact that after yesterday she was happy to be alive and relieved her ankle was feeling so much better. She hummed a song she'd heard on the radio a few days ago as she descended the staircase and walked toward the kitchen.

Mrs. Knight, dressed in her nurse's uniform, stood at the sink drinking a cup of coffee. She smiled when Claire came into the room. "Good morning. I hoped you would wake up before I left."

Claire pulled a cup from the cabinet and poured herself a cup of coffee. "I'm glad you're still here. I wanted to thank you for letting me stay here last night."

Mrs. Knight rinsed out her cup and set it in the dishwasher. "You know you're always welcome here. I wish I had time to sit and talk with you, but I have to be at work in thirty minutes. I think you know where everything is, so help yourself to breakfast."

"Thanks," Claire said as she slid into a chair at the table. "Where is everybody this morning?"

"Adam has gone to his apartment to shower and put on some clean clothes. His father has gone down to the agency. With Jessica out and Adam working on your case, he thought Lucas might be shorthanded today."

Claire frowned. "I hope it hasn't inconvenienced everyone with Adam helping me out."

She waved her hand in dismissal. "Of course it hasn't. That's what family is for, to help each other when we're needed. And that's what we consider you, Claire. You're family."

"This has always felt like my second home. I've missed it since I've been in Nashville."

Mrs. Knight came around the table and gave her a swift hug. "Well, you're here now, and we're all glad. Don't stay away so long anymore."

Claire fought back the tears that stung her eyes. "I won't."

Mrs. Knight picked up her purse and pulled her car keys from inside. She started to walk away but stopped. "Oh, I almost forgot. Jessica left some clothes over here last week, and I laundered them for her. There's a pair of jeans and a sweatshirt in her closet. Feel free to wear them today. That way you won't have to use up time going home to change."

Claire swallowed the last of her coffee and stood. "Thanks. I hope Jessica and I still wear the same size."

"I'm sure you do. The two of you have been wearing each other's clothes ever since you were in elementary school. I hope you and Adam can get a lead on these men you're looking for today."

"So do I. And thanks again for letting me stay."

After putting her dishes in the dishwasher, she hurried back upstairs so she'd be dressed and ready to go when Adam returned. As she climbed the stairs, she couldn't help remembering the time they had spent together the night before. Then she shook the thought from her head and turned her thoughts to finding Peter Willis and James Lester before they tried again to kill her and Adam.

When she came downstairs thirty minutes later, Adam sat at the kitchen table with a cup of coffee. His gaze swept over her as she entered the room, and her skin warmed. "You look like you're ready for the day."

"I am. What do you think we should do today?"

"I've been trying to decide. Have you talked with Peter's wife yet?"

"Yes. I went by there last week, but she had no idea where he could be. She said he hadn't contacted her since he was released on bond."

"Did you think she was telling the truth?"

Claire thought about that for a moment. "At the time I thought so, but with all that's happened, I don't know. She had to know about the cabin in Mississippi, but she didn't tell me about it. If she had really wanted to help me, I'd think she'd have given me some information about Peter. But she didn't."

Adam pushed up from the table. "Then let's go see her this morning. Then we can decide what our next step will be."

"Let me get my jacket and purse, and I'll be ready to go."

"I'll wait for you in the car."

A few minutes later she walked out the front door and joined Adam in the car. She fastened her seat belt, and he backed out of the driveway. "Which way do I go to get to Peter's house?"

"They live in one of those upscale neighborhoods down on Mud Island."

Adam's eyebrows arched, and he gave a low whistle. "The houses down there are really expensive. A bank loan officer must make a lot more money than I thought."

"It really is a beautiful home, and the furnishings are out of this world. I could hardly carry on a conversation with Mrs. Willis. All I wanted to do was drool over the way her house was decorated."

He chuckled and pulled off their side street into the busy morning traffic. "I can hardly wait to see it."

Thirty minutes later they pulled to a stop in front of a rambling two-story house on a shaded lot. A wrought-iron fence separated the lawn from the sidewalk. Jessica glanced over at Adam. "What do you think?"

He exhaled a long breath. "I definitely had no idea how much Peter must have made at the bank."

She laughed and climbed from the car. "Let's go surprise Mrs. Willis."

A flagstone walkway stretched from the fence's gate to the house, and they strode toward the front porch. At the entrance Adam pushed the button for the doorbell, and they waited.

It was opened by a young woman in a maid's uniform. She smiled at them. "May I help you?"

"We're here to see Mrs. Willis," Adam said.

The woman's smile didn't falter. "I'm sorry. Mrs. Willis is working out right now. Could you come back later?"

Adam shook his head. "I'm afraid not. Please tell her we're the bounty hunters who are searching for her husband."

The maid's eyes grew large. "Bounty hunters?"

"Yes, and I imagine the police will be showing up here sometime today to ask her some questions about him, so it would probably be a good idea for her to talk to us first."

The woman glanced over her shoulder and then back to them. She stepped back and opened the door wider. "Come in. You can wait in the living room, and I'll go get her."

She ushered Adam and Claire into the room where Claire had sat the last time she'd been here, and they took seats on a brocade sofa. Within minutes Mrs. Willis came storming into the room. She wore a pair of black ankle-length leggings and a matching tank top. A sweatband held her hair back from her face.

Her eyes flashed when she spotted Claire. "What are you doing here? I told you last week I haven't heard from my husband. I have no idea where he is, but I suspect he's left the country by now."

"Not unless he left yesterday, Mrs. Willis. He tried to kill me the night before last," Claire said.

Her eyes grew large. "Tried to kill you? What are you talking about?"

As Claire relayed the events of the past two days, Mrs. Willis's face grew more somber. "So your husband is a vicious killer, and if you know anything about him, you'd better tell us. If we bring him in and then find out you helped protect him, you can be charged with harboring a fugitive."

Mrs. Willis leaned forward and glared at Claire. "I don't know anything about what my husband has been up to. I told the police he was at home the night Lance Morgan was murdered, but they didn't believe me. They wanted to close that case fast, and they picked my husband to take the fall for it."

"You're quick to take up for your husband, Mrs. Willis," Adam said.

"Of course I am. He's my husband, and I love him."

"And you think he's innocent?"

Mrs. Willis straightened her back and frowned. "I know Peter better than anyone does. We've been married ten years and during that time he's been nothing but a good and kind husband."

Claire scooted to the edge of her seat and stared at the woman. "Then why do you think he hasn't contacted you? It seems to me if you were as close as you say, he'd want to talk to you."

The woman took a deep breath and stood. "He hasn't contacted me because he knows I'm being harassed by the police and bounty hunters who are intent on bringing him in." She narrowed her eyes and took a step toward them. "I've heard about people like you. It's dead or alive, isn't it? As long as you get your money, you don't care."

Claire jumped to her feet. "When your husband jumped bail, he left my father's business owing a lot of money to the court, but that's not the only reason I want him returned to custody. Your husband murdered my father in cold blood, and I intend to see that he pays for it."

Mrs. Willis stared at Claire for a moment before she let out a soft chuckle. "You're crazy if you think my husband would kill anybody. Now I want both of you out of my house." She turned her head and called out, "Marie, our guests are leaving now. Would you please show them to the door?"

As if she'd been waiting right outside the doorway, the maid reappeared. "Yes, ma'am."

Adam took Claire by the arm, and they followed Marie toward the front door. They were just about to step outside when they heard footsteps on the entry's hardwood floors. They turned to see Mrs. Willis standing a few feet behind the maid.

"Marie, in the future if these two come back here, they are not to be invited in. Do you understand?"

The maid bobbed her head up and down. "Yes, ma'am."

Claire bristled and was about to offer a retort, but Adam tightened his grip on her arm and propelled her out the front door. Once outside, Marie closed the door.

Claire shook free of Adam's hold on her and clenched her fists at her side. "Can you believe that woman? She's married to a murderer, and she acts like we're the bad guys."

Adam chuckled. "Get used to it, Claire. A lot of people have little respect for bounty hunters, but the job we do helps protect the innocent victims that these criminals will prey on if they're not caught and returned to jail. If you're going to work in this profession, you're going to have to develop a thick skin."

"I'm not sure I'm going to keep doing this after we find Peter. That librarian's job is looking sweeter all the time. Coping with a school full of active adolescents who experience frequent mood swings is nothing compared to being shot at and almost killed in a hit-and-run."

He threw back his head and laughed. "I can see how your old life could be so attractive right now." He leaned closer and grinned. "But just think of the fun you'd be missing if you weren't on the trail of a fugitive."

Claire inhaled the scent of Adam's aftershave as he stepped closer to her, and she swallowed the longing that filled her. Once she had thought she'd never love anyone like she did him. Then that had all changed.

But we've gotten past that, she argued with herself. All she could do was what she had told him. She would be his friend. That would be it. Nothing more.

She smiled and inclined her head toward the car at the curb. "Speaking of fugitives, it's time we got back to work. Where do we go from here?"

"Maybe it's time we paid a visit to the Serenity Wellness Spa outside of town. What do you think?"

She shrugged. "Sounds good to me."

They headed toward the car but had only taken a few steps when Claire's cell phone rang. She pulled it from her pocket. "Hello."

"Miss Walker?"

"Yes."

"This is Detective Barnes with the Memphis Police Department. I was one of the officers who spoke with you at Jessica Knight's apartment after the break-in."

She smiled. "Oh, yes, Detective Barnes. I remember you."

"I thought I would let you know we found a car registered to James Lester."

Her mouth gaped open in surprise. "You have? Where was it?"

"It was in the parking lot of an abandoned factory in North Memphis."

"That's wonderful. It's probably the same car that tried to run Adam Knight and me down in a bank parking lot yesterday."

"I saw that report, and this car has the same license plate number that the witness at the bank gave to police."

She turned to Adam and whispered, "The police have found James Lester's car."

"That's great," he mouthed.

Claire spoke into the phone again. "Did you find anything in the car that might give a clue to James's whereabouts?"

A long sigh came over the phone. "That's what I wanted to let you know."

Her eyebrows arched. "Oh, what is it?"

"I'm at the medical examiner's office right now. There were two bodies inside the car."

EIGHT

Out of the corner of her eye Claire watched Adam as he hunched over the steering wheel and maneuvered the car through the traffic on the bridge that linked Mud Island to downtown Memphis. He hadn't said anything since they'd rushed off from the Willis home. She noticed the muscle in his jaw flex as he chewed on his bottom lip. She'd often seen that look when he was lost in thought about something. She'd found out years ago that it was better to leave him to his thoughts when he was like that. She turned her head and stared out the window.

He kept silent until he turned onto Poplar Avenue. "Are you okay?" he asked.

His unexpected question startled her, and she swiveled in her seat to stare at him. "I'm fine. How about you? You seemed like you were in another world."

"Sorry," he said. "I was just thinking about what Detective Barnes said. Didn't he give you any idea who the two dead people are?"

"No, he said that he knew we were searching for James and Peter and that after the break-in at Jessica's he thought we might want to come down to the medical examiner's office to offer a positive identification.

That makes me think it must be Peter and James. Who else could it be?"

"I don't know. But at this point let's not speculate until we get there."

She nodded. "You're right. It may be two unlucky people who happened to cross the pair's path." A bitter taste poured into her mouth at the thought of where they were headed, and she swallowed. "Have you ever been to the medical examiner's office before?"

He nodded. "I've been there quite a few times." He glanced at her. "What about you?"

She shook her head. "No."

"Are you worried about going there?"

She fidgeted in her seat and pulled her seat belt tighter. "No. I just don't know what to expect. But come to think of it, the past few days have been a big change from my normal everyday life. I just never expected to be making a trip to the medical examiner's office."

He reached over and placed his hand on top of hers. "Don't worry. I'll be with you." He darted a glance at her and grinned. "And if I see you're about to faint, I'll *try* to catch you before you hit the floor."

She pulled her hand free of his and swatted at him. "Try? Thanks, friend."

He laughed and turned his attention back to the traffic, but a small smile still pulled at his mouth. This was the Adam she liked better, the teasing one who made her heart race. Not the brooding one who retreated into the places in his mind that he'd never revealed to anyone. He'd almost opened up to her that night six years ago, but never again until their conversation in the kitchen last night.

She dropped her gaze and stared at the floorboard.

Even though they'd experienced some terrifying moments during the past few days, being with Adam had made her happier than she'd been in a long time. What she needed to do now was concentrate on what she'd come to realize. He wasn't an enemy like she'd let herself believe for the past six years.

She had to admit that what she'd known in her heart all along was true, Adam was a good man. He loved his family, and he cared about his friends. And she realized that he didn't dislike her as she had thought, but he really wanted to be her friend. If he could only learn to accept the love God wanted to give him, he would be on his way to learning how to live with the memories that still haunted him. She hoped he could come to see how wrong he was about God's love for him.

The car turned into the parking lot of the new facility that housed the medical examiner's office, and Adam pulled to a stop. He waved his hand in the direction of the brick building. "This is it. As you can see, there isn't anything frightening about it."

"No, there isn't. Still, I'm glad you're with me."

He let his gaze drift over her face, and he smiled. "So am I."

They climbed from the car and walked toward the building. They stepped to the front door, but before Adam could reach for the handle, the door opened. Detective Barnes stood in the hallway inside. "I was waiting for you. Thanks for coming."

They stepped into the entry and stopped beside the policeman. Adam reached out and shook hands with him. "We were glad to come. Have you identified the bodies found in the car?"

He nodded and looked at Claire. "I'm sorry if I was

evasive when I was on the phone, but I was trying to talk with you and catch what the medical examiner was saying to my partner."

"I understand, but tell us about the bodies inside the car."

Detective Barnes took a deep breath. "Two officers on patrol spotted the car in the parking lot at about five o'clock this morning. When they looked inside, they saw James Lester slumped over the steering wheel. He'd died of a gunshot wound."

Claire gasped and brought her hand to her throat. "Did he die from the wound he received when I shot him at Jessica's apartment?"

"No. From what I understand, he did have a wound on his leg that had been bandaged. But he died after being shot in the head."

Claire sighed in relief. "Thank goodness. Even if he did try to kill me, I wouldn't want to be the cause of his death. But you said there were two bodies in the car."

"Yes. After finding Lester, they opened the trunk, and there was another body in it. Since there was no identification on the victim, they didn't know who he was."

"So it wasn't Peter Willis?" Adam asked.

Detective Barnes shook his head. "No. The bodies were brought here, and they started checking to see if there had been any reports of a missing person turned in overnight. It turned out there had been. A woman reported that her husband never came home after work. She said that he had never done anything like that before. So we called her, and she came down. She gave us a positive identification of her husband's body a few minutes ago. I thought you might know him, but we have his name now."

"What is the victim's name?" Claire asked.

"Jonathan Fields."

Claire gasped and looked at Adam, whose face had turned pale. "Jonathan Fields who worked at the bank with Peter Willis?"

A surprised look crossed the detective's face. "How did you know him?"

"We talked to him at the bank right before James's car tried to run us down. James must have seen Jonathan talking to us and decided to kill him. Jonathan told us he had information about some trouble between Peter and Lance Morgan, who was murdered."

"That's right," Detective Barnes said. "He was a potential witness in the case."

Claire closed her eyes and shook her head. "Oh, no. Was Jonathan murdered because he talked to us?"

Adam grabbed her shoulder and gave her a gentle shake. "No, Claire," he said. "Peter probably had him targeted from the very beginning of this case. He knew Jonathan was going to testify, and as we've found out in the past few days, Peter doesn't want to leave any witnesses."

"Mr. Knight's right, Miss Walker," Detective Barnes said. "We don't have any evidence to support our theory yet, but we believe Peter probably killed James after they killed Jonathan. After all, James had botched the attempt on your life at Jessica's apartment and then again at the bank. We may know for sure when the report comes back from ballistics. If the bullets from Lance Morgan's body and James Lester's are from the same gun, we have reasonable belief to charge Peter with both murders."

"If my father was killed with the same gun, Willis could be linked to his murder, too," Claire added.

Detective Barnes nodded. "We'll check on that. If they are the same, we can charge Willis with all three murders."

Adam exhaled a deep breath. "We have to find him first."

Detective Barnes looked at him. "I thought you were hired to go after James Lester."

"I was. Now that he's dead I'm off that case. But I'll continue to help Claire look for Peter Willis."

Detective Barnes sighed. "All I can tell you two is to be careful. Peter Willis is a murderer, and if he killed Lester, he must not have any loyalty to his friends, much less his enemies."

"We will," Claire said. "But before we go, I wanted to ask you about Jonathan's wife. Is she still here?"

He nodded. "Yes, she's sitting in that room down the hall on the right. I think she's waiting for someone to join her."

"Would it be okay if I talked to her?"

"If you want to question her about her husband's death, you won't have any luck. We've already talked to her enough to know that she is completely in the dark about why anyone would want to kill her husband. Evidently he hadn't told her he had talked to us about the argument he overheard between Lance and Peter."

Claire shook her head. "No, I don't want to ask her any questions. I only want to offer her my condolences."

"Then go ahead. I have to get back to headquarters, but thanks for coming. If you two find out anything about Willis, let us know."

Adam stuck out his hand. "We will."

The detective shook Adam's hand. "Tell Jessica hello for me. We still miss her at the station. I think my partner, Ryan, really does. He worked with her before she quit to work with you."

Adam nodded. "I'll tell her."

Detective Barnes shook Claire's hand and then walked out the front door. She watched him go before she took a deep breath. "I'll be back in a minute. I want to see Mrs. Fields."

"I'll wait for you here."

"I won't be long," she called over her shoulder as she strode toward the room the detective had pointed out.

As Claire stepped into the room, she spotted a young woman sitting alone on a couch. She leaned forward, her elbows propped on her knees. She clutched a tissue in her hands and pressed it against her eyes. Her shoulders shook, and a muffled sob seemed to echo in the silent room.

Claire stopped in front of her. "Mrs. Fields?"

The woman jerked upright in her seat and stared at Claire. "Yes?"

Claire's heart sank at the sight of the woman's grief-stricken face and her red eyes. "My name is Claire Walker. I wanted to come in and tell you how sorry I am about your husband's death."

The young woman dabbed at her eyes with the tissue. "Are you with the police?"

"No. I'm really a school librarian, but right now I'm working on a case with a fugitive recovery agent to bring in two men who jumped bail. One of them was James Lester."

Her eyebrows arched. "The other man who was in the car?"

"Yes."

A puzzled look crossed her face. "This is all so confusing to me. Jonathan never mentioned anyone named James Lester to me. The police told me there's a warrant out for his arrest on another charge."

"Yes. That's why my friend and I were trying to find him. I wish we had before he crossed paths with your husband."

"I do, too." The woman's body shook as she choked back a sob. "So you were looking for this criminal. But did you know my husband?"

"I met him at the bank once. I thought he was a very nice young man. I wanted to tell you how sorry I am about his death."

Fresh tears ran down the woman's face. "Thank you, Miss… I'm sorry. I've already forgotten your last name."

"Walker, but just call me Claire. I understand you not remembering my name. You have your mind on other things right now."

The woman scooted over and motioned for Claire to sit beside her. "My name is Molly. I appreciate your coming in here. I assume you want to ask me questions about the other man found in the car, but I'm at a loss to understand what Jonathan was doing with him."

Claire shook her head. "No, I don't want to ask you about him. I only wanted to check on you and see if there's anything I can do for you. Can we drive you home? Call a family member or friend?"

"We don't have family here. Jonathan and I moved here from Georgia where we grew up. Both of our families live there, as do most of our friends. But we do have a wonderful pastor here in Memphis, and I've called for him to come. He and his wife are on their way."

"That's good to hear. I live in Nashville, but I lost my father here recently. I don't know what I would have done without his pastor to help me through those days. I'm glad to know that you're a believer."

Molly's eyes lit up. "Oh, I am, and so was Jonathan." She placed her hand on her stomach. "We found out a few weeks ago that we're going to have a baby, and Jonathan was so happy. He grew up in a faith-filled home, and that's what he wanted for our child." Suddenly her eyes darkened and filled with tears. "Now he'll never know his child. How can I face raising our baby without him?"

Molly covered her eyes with her hands as the tears streamed down her face. Claire reached out and put her arm around her shoulders, and Molly collapsed against her. Claire sat there until Molly appeared spent from her tears.

"It's going to be all right," Claire whispered. "God will help you get through this."

Molly straightened and looked at her. "I know that, but right now it's hard to bear."

"And it will be for a long time, but that doesn't mean God's forgotten you. He's right there with you, taking every step alongside you. He'll give you the strength to make it through each day. And as you do, you'll find that each one will get easier."

"I'll try to remember that."

Claire took a deep breath. "And remember this, too. God has already blessed you in a special way. He's given you Jonathan's baby so that you'll always have a part of him with you. Isn't that wonderful?"

Molly's eyes sparkled with tears, but she smiled. "I hadn't thought of it that way." She reached out and grasped Claire's hand. "Thank you for coming in to see me. You've helped me so much."

Claire smiled and pushed to her feet. "I hope so. And I'll be praying for you, Molly. I know God is going to bless you and your child beyond anything you can imagine at the moment."

Molly stood and wrapped her arms around Claire in a hug. "I hope we meet again."

"Maybe we will. Now I have to go. You take care of yourself."

"You, too," Molly said as she sank back onto the couch.

Claire turned to leave the room but paused at the sight of Adam standing in the doorway. He glanced from Molly to her before he whirled around and strode down the hall. Claire hurried from the room and into the hall just as he shoved the front door open with all his strength and stormed outside.

She stood there, not knowing what to do. Had Adam overheard her conversation with Molly? Just because he didn't share her belief in God was no reason for him to get angry because she spoke about it to someone else. Someone who was hurting and needed to hold on to her faith to get her through the trying days ahead.

Adam might not realize it, but he needed that same help. She hoped that what he'd overheard hadn't made him more determined than ever to ignore the need for God in his life.

The front door slammed shut, and Claire squared her shoulders. If Adam was angry with her, it was better she find out now instead of later. She clenched her fists at her side. She needed to get to the car right away.

Adam jerked the car door open and crawled into the driver's seat. He grasped the steering wheel with both hands and squeezed. His heart pounded, and his chest felt as if it was about to explode. What was the matter with him?

He'd been fine until he decided to see what was keeping Claire so long, and he'd stepped up to the door just in time to hear her and Jonathan Fields's wife talking about faith. He'd listened for a few minutes without being affected until the woman had asked how she was going to bear living with her husband's death.

Claire's answer about how God would help had stunned him. *He's right there with you, taking every step alongside you. He'll give you the strength to make it through each day. And as you do, you'll find that each one will get easier,* she'd said.

He closed his eyes as the memory of watching his best friend take his last breath on the horrible day the roadside bomb had shattered his body. He remembered how the corpsmen had worked to revive him, but in the end it had done no good.

One more useless death in battle. And now Jonathan Fields had become another who hadn't deserved to die. Would his wife gain consolation from what Claire had said to her?

The door on the passenger side opened, and he turned toward Claire as she climbed inside. A small frown wrinkled her forehead. "Adam, are you okay?"

"Yeah." He put a shaky hand on the ignition, but she reached over and stopped him.

"What's the matter? You looked so angry when I saw you in the hallway. Then you rushed out of the building like a madman. Did I do something to make you angry?"

He sighed and raked his hand through his hair. "No.

It wasn't you. It's me. I overheard what you were saying, and I had to get out of there."

"Why?"

He thought for a moment before he answered. "You know that I grew up with parents who love God. They tried to teach their children about Him. But when I went into the army, I began to wonder how God could let such horrible things happen to the men and women around me. What kind of God does that? Let mothers and fathers be killed?"

"Like Jonathan Fields?"

"Exactly. I don't understand. God must not exist or He would have taken care of them."

Claire reached out her hand to him. "Everyone dies, Adam. And it's not always at the time that we would choose. We have to have faith and believe God will help us get through the hard times that come with such experiences."

"Yeah, getting cut down in battle is definitely a hard time for the one hit."

She didn't say anything for a moment. "Were any of your friends who died believers?"

"Yes."

"Then I'm sure they were comforted by God's presence."

Adam glared at her. "You seem to have an answer for everything. Except one. When you come right down to it, you can't prove to me God is real."

A sad smile pulled at her mouth. "I'm sorry to hear you say that, but I wonder something."

"What?"

She leaned closer. "If you're so sure that God doesn't exist, then why do you get so angry and upset when you think about it? If I didn't believe, like you say you don't, I wouldn't waste my energy giving it a second thought. I'd just live it up every day without getting all angry about people who don't agree with me."

He slammed his hand against the steering wheel. "I'm not angry."

A smile curled her lips, and she reached over and covered his hand with hers. "You could sure fool me, but I don't want to argue with you. It all comes down to whether or not we choose to believe. The Bible tells us, 'Faith is the substance of things hoped for, the evidence of things not seen.' I'm praying that you will find it in your heart to accept what God offers, but you're the one who has to make the decision."

He looked down at her hand covering his and then to her. His heart thudded at the glow on her face. He'd never seen her more beautiful, and in that moment he wished he could be more like her. He'd never known anyone like her, and she affected him in a way that no other woman ever had.

He wrapped his fingers around hers. "I'm sorry. There's no excuse for my behavior. Maybe I'm feeling guilty about Jonathan's death. I'm glad you talked with his wife. I'm sure it helped her."

"I hope so. But I want to help you, too."

"Sometimes I think I'm beyond being helped."

"That's not true, Adam. God loves you. But you're the one who has to make the choice about whether or not to believe in Him. Just think about what I've said."

He reached out and tucked a strand of hair behind her ear, then let his index finger trail down her cheek. "You make me want to be a better person, Claire. I wish

I could see things through your eyes. I don't know if I can, but I'll think about what you said."

She smiled. "That's all I'm asking you to do."

He pulled his hand away from her face and took a deep breath before he reached out and turned the ignition. "Now I'm going to take you to your father's house so you can pack a bag. While you were talking with Mrs. Fields, I called Serenity Wellness Spa and booked us each a room starting tomorrow. Maybe we can find out if Peter has connections to the spa other than the loan from the bank."

Her eyes grew wide, and she shook her head. "Adam, this sounds expensive. I can't afford to stay there."

"Oh, yes, you can. I'll pay for it through the Knight Agency."

"But finding Peter isn't going to help your business in any way. He's my responsibility."

He paused before putting the car in gear and scowled at her. "Are we going to argue again? I want to find Peter as much as you do, and I'm going to pay for us to stay at the spa. Okay?"

Her mouth opened, but she didn't speak for a moment. Then she shrugged. "Okay. If you say so."

"I do. And while you're packing, pick out your prettiest dress to bring along. Something that will complement those big blue eyes of yours. After all we've been through in the past few days, I think we deserve some fun. I'm taking you to the swankiest restaurant in East Memphis tonight for dinner."

She batted her eyelashes at him and grinned. "Why, Mr. Knight, are you asking me out on a date?"

His skin grew warm, and he swallowed. "I guess I am. Is that all right with you?"

"I can't think of anything I'd rather do."

A warm feeling curled in the pit of his stomach. "Me, either."

He stared at her for a minute. A voice in his head urged him to reach across the seat and pull her into his arms, but she probably wouldn't like that. He shook the thought from his head and pulled the car into the early-afternoon traffic.

NINE

Claire closed her eyes with pleasure as the last bite of crème brûlée slid down her throat. When she opened her eyes, Adam was staring at her across the table. Her face warmed, and she glanced around the crowded restaurant.

"Did anyone see me enjoy that last morsel of a fabulous dessert?"

Adam picked up his coffee cup and stared at her over the rim. "I don't think so. But from the way you've eaten tonight, I'd say you've really enjoyed the food."

"Oh, I have. Thank you for bringing me here, Adam. I could never afford this place on my salary. If the bounty hunter business pays enough to afford places like this and the spa where we're going tomorrow, then I may decide to change my mind and stay in Memphis."

He took a sip of coffee and set his cup back down. "We'd all like to see you stay in Memphis, but I don't know about you taking on the job of a bounty hunter."

She pushed her plate out of her way and crossed her arms in front of her on the table. "I've learned a lot from you in the past few days. I'm sure by the time we catch up with Peter, I'll be a seasoned bounty hunter."

He chuckled and shook his head. "Don't count on it. It takes a while to get used to this kind of life."

"Jessica seems to like it fine."

"Yes, but Jessica's had a lot of law enforcement training that has helped her. I don't think a librarian's job offers that much practical experience for chasing down bail jumpers."

Claire couldn't help but laugh. "You may have a point. But what I lack in skill I make up for in determination."

He arched his eyebrows and nodded. "You can say that again."

She was about to respond when an unfamiliar voice sounded behind her. "Well, look who's here. I didn't think you were the dating type, Knight. Now I see you out on the town. From all the talking and laughter that's been coming from your table, I'd say you're having a good time."

Claire glanced up at the large bald-headed man who stopped next to their table and smiled down at them. When he reached out to shake hands with Adam, she almost gasped at the number of rings he wore. She'd never seen so many diamonds on one person in her life.

Adam grasped the man's hand and smiled. "Wes, good to see you."

Wes glanced at Claire, then winked at Adam. "It looks like you've been holding out on me. I had no idea you had such a pretty friend."

Adam chuckled. "Claire, this is Wes Stratton. Wes, Claire Walker. She's a longtime friend of the family."

Claire's forehead wrinkled. "Stratton? Are you the owner of the Bond Squad Bail Bond Company?"

"I sure am, Miss Walker. I hope you've never had to use our services."

She shook her head. "No, but I'm running my father's business at present, Walker's Bail Bonds."

The smile disappeared from Wes's face. "So you're Henry Walker's daughter? I was so sorry to hear of your father's death. I hope you got the flowers we sent."

"Yes. They were beautiful. Thank you."

He narrowed his eyes and stared at her for a moment. "So you're running your father's business?"

"Right now I am."

An amused look flashed on his face. "A bail bond business is not the place for a pretty woman like you. Have you given any thought to selling?"

Claire clenched her fists in her lap and struggled to control the anger that surged through her. "Mr. Stratton, my father told me that you tried repeatedly to buy his business, and that you had already bought up a lot of the smaller ones. But he wasn't interested in selling and neither am I. If you're looking to have a monopoly on the business, I think you're going to have a rough go of it in a city as large as Memphis."

He laid a hand on his chest and widened his eyes as if he was surprised at her outburst. "Why, Miss Walker, I was only trying to help your father get out of a financial disaster, and I'd like to do the same for you. But if you're not interested, I won't approach you again."

"Thank you."

Wes glanced over at Adam, who had remained silent. "By the way, Adam, I received a call from the police that James Lester's body was discovered in his car this morning. The money I forfeited to the court when he jumped bail will be returned, and I intend to pay your fee even though you didn't bring him in."

"Thanks, Wes," Adam said, "but you don't have to…"

Wes held up his hand to stop him. "I insist. The Bond Squad doesn't want any bounty hunter to lose money on jobs they perform for us." He glanced at Claire. "That's one of the things that sets us apart from other companies, Miss Walker. I hope you'll be able to do the same."

Adam pushed to his feet and stuck out his hand before Claire could answer. "I'll send you a bill."

"See that you do." He shook Adam's hand, nodded to her and walked away from the table.

When he'd gone, Adam sat back down and glanced at Claire. "Are you all right?"

Claire watched Wes Stratton as he walked from the restaurant's dining room. "There's something about that man I don't trust."

"Do you think you might be influenced by the fact that he tried to buy your father's business?"

"No. My father didn't trust him, either." When he disappeared into the lobby, she shook her head. "But maybe you're right, and my father's opinion influenced me. Anyway, I don't think this was the appropriate time to bring up buying my business."

Before Adam could respond, the waitress stopped at their table. "Can I get you anything else?"

"Just the check," Adam said.

Claire pushed up from the table as the waitress left to get their bill. "I'm going to the ladies' room. I'll be back in a few minutes."

She grabbed her purse and headed to the lobby where she'd seen signs indicating the restrooms. As she exited the dining room, she spotted Wes Stratton with his cell phone clamped against his ear going out the door. She eased over to the door and pushed it open a few inches so she could peer outside.

The way he gestured wildly with his free hand as he talked and stormed down the sidewalk toward the side of the building made her wonder what could have upset him so much. Probably something to do with his business.

She turned and entered the hallway where the restrooms were located. At the ladies' room she stopped and thought about Wes again. The events of the past few days had made her view things she might have dismissed a week ago in a different light now.

After all, Wes had a link to James Lester. It might only be that he had paid his bail, but then it could be something more. If she didn't check it out, she would never know.

She glanced at the door with the exit sign above it at the end of the hall. It wouldn't hurt to see if she could find out anything. She hurried to the door and pushed it open a few inches so she could see outside.

Wes Stratton, still on the phone, paced up and down the alley at the rear of the building. A Dumpster sat near him. Claire eased through the door and into the shadows next to the building. Holding her breath, she tiptoed closer until she reached the Dumpster and crouched down behind it.

"I don't care what you thought!" she heard Wes say. "I told you I'd have the money for you, and I will. I just need more time."

A chill rippled up Claire's spine, and she realized for the first time she'd left the restaurant without her coat. She shivered and berated herself for following Wes Stratton. From what she'd heard, his phone call was nothing more than a bill collector trying to get him to pay a debt.

"Yes, I know you're charging interest!" Wes said.

"But it's going to be hard to get hold of that much money by tomorrow. All I'm asking for is a few days more."

Now she really wished she'd stayed inside. She shouldn't be listening to a man beg a creditor for more time. She rose to a squat and was about to try to scoot back into the shadows when she froze in place at his next words.

"Look, Willis, don't threaten me. It wouldn't be good for your business if something happened to me."

Claire clamped her hand over her mouth to keep from gasping out loud. Peter Willis? That was the person on the phone threatening Wes Stratton?

Wes's groan drifted on the night air. "Okay, you're right. We can work this out. I'll see you the day after tomorrow at Serenity. And, Willis, don't call me again."

Claire huddled close to the Dumpster as Wes made his way from the alley back to the front of the restaurant. She waited a few minutes in hopes that he would be gone by the time she reentered the restaurant.

After what seemed an eternity, she pushed to her feet and took a tentative step away from the Dumpster and into the shadows. Before she could move a sharp voice crackled in the darkness.

"What are you doing out here?"

Claire gave a squeal of surprise, doubled up her fist and swung at the figure in the shadows. Before she could land a blow, the man ducked, grabbed her around the waist and hoisted her over his shoulder.

Claire writhed and kicked at him as her fists pounded him in the back. With a groan Adam loosened his grip on Claire and stood her in front of him. He grabbed her fist as she swung at him once more.

"Claire, will you cut it out?" he yelled.

She stilled and sucked in her breath. "Adam?"

"Yes, it's Adam."

She threw her arms around his waist and laid her cheek against his chest. "Oh, Adam, I'm so glad to see you. I thought Wes Stratton had found me."

For a moment he stood still, uncertain what to do. Then he felt her body tremble, and he wrapped his arms around her and pulled her closer. "Claire, what are you talking about?"

She pulled back and stared up at him. "I was on my way to the ladies' room and I saw Wes on his cell phone."

Once she started talking, the words poured from her mouth. By the time she got to the end of her story, his mouth was gaping in shock. When she finished, he took her by the shoulders and stared into her eyes.

"Claire, what were you thinking? You should have come and gotten me. I would have followed him."

"By the time I told you, he would probably have been through with his conversation, and we wouldn't know that he owes Peter Willis money."

"But still, you could have been hurt."

"Well, I'm not," she said. "Unless you count the fact that you scared about ten years off my life." She put her hands on her hips and arched an eyebrow. "How did you know I was out here?"

"When you didn't come back to the table, I got worried. I waited in the lobby a few minutes and then I asked the hostess if she had seen you. She said she'd seen you leaving through the exit at the end of the hall. When I opened the door, I saw Wes walking from the alley and watched him get in his car. Then I went looking for you and saw you behind the Dumpster. I didn't mean to scare you."

She hugged her arms around her waist and shivered. "And I didn't mean to worry you by taking off like that. I won't do it again."

He leaned toward her until their noses almost touched. "See that you don't."

She smiled. "I won't. Now, can we go get my coat? I'm freezing out here."

He took off his jacket and draped it around her shoulders. "Wear this until we get inside. Then we're going to my parents' home. I think you've had enough excitement for tonight."

She hugged the jacket around her and stared up at him. "We're still going to Serenity tomorrow, aren't we?"

"Yes. I need to go into the office for a few hours in the morning, but I'll be back by lunch. I thought we'd leave for Serenity in the early afternoon."

They started toward the restaurant, and Claire looked up at him. "Adam, why do you think Wes would owe Peter money?"

"I have no idea, but I think the answer probably lies at the Serenity Wellness Center. And we need to find out what it is."

A few hours later Adam sat in the kitchen of his parents' home as he drank a cup of coffee and replayed the events of the night in his head. Although he'd been concerned when he found out why Claire had left the restaurant, he had to give her credit. When she set her mind to something, she couldn't be distracted. By following Wes Stratton she'd uncovered a piece of information that might be useful in catching up to Peter Willis.

At least they knew he'd be coming to Serenity, and they would be there, too.

He smiled as he remembered how beautiful Claire had looked tonight at dinner and how good it had felt when she put her arms around him and laid her head on his chest. The truth that he'd tried to deny for six years filled his mind, and he closed his eyes. He'd been in love with Claire for years, but he'd done everything he could to conceal the truth from himself and everybody around him.

The memory of how he'd hurt her and the anger she'd felt toward him for years returned. He gritted his teeth and struck the table with his fist.

"No!"

It would never work out. Even though she said she'd forgiven him, all she wanted from him was friendship. The sooner he accepted that, the better off he'd be.

"What's going on in here?"

Startled at the sound of his mother's voice, Adam glanced up as she entered the room. He straightened in the chair and picked up his cup. "Nothing. I'm having a cup of coffee before I go to bed."

She slid into the chair across from him and frowned as she studied him. "Adam, I've always been able to tell when you're upset about something, and I know you are now. What's the matter? If there's a problem with the business, I'm sure your father will be glad…"

He held up his hand to stop her. "No, Mom. It's not the business. It's something else."

She crossed her arms on the table in front of her and leaned forward. "Then it must be Claire."

He frowned and fidgeted in his chair, then picked up his cup again. "Where did you get that idea?"

She sighed. "Oh, Adam. Why do you have to make everything so difficult? I see the way you look at her, and I see the way she looks at you. I know you had some problems in the past, but those seem to be resolved. Why are you so afraid to let her know how you feel?"

He curled his fingers around the coffee cup and stared down at the liquid inside for a moment before he responded. "Claire is a wonderful woman, Mom. But she doesn't need me. She needs a man who believes like she does. Or, as she would say, a man who has faith that God loves him. I'm not that man."

His heart pricked at the tears that pooled in his mother's eyes, but she blinked them away. "Your father and I would like to see you become that man. We pray every day that you will. You're never going to be happy until you step out of the way and let God take control of your life."

A sad smile pulled at his mouth. "Claire said basically the same thing to me. Have you two been talking?"

"No. We both want you to recognize what you're missing in life by your refusal to let God into your heart." She reached across the table and covered his hand with hers. "But your father and I, and Claire also, can't do it for you. You have to come to the point where you accept God. We're all praying you'll do that."

He brought her hand to his lips and kissed it. "Thanks, Mom. I love you."

"I love you, too."

He pushed his chair back, rose and reached for his cup. "I have a lot to do tomorrow, so I'd better get in bed."

"Leave your cup. I think I'll have a cup, too. Then I'll clean up. You go on to bed."

He walked around the table and kissed her on the cheek. "Night, Mom."

"Good night. Sleep well."

As he left the kitchen and climbed the staircase, he thought of the things his mother had said to him. Outside Claire's closed door, he stopped a moment and thought how his mother had echoed her thoughts.

The angry voice in his head he'd known for so many years whispered that they didn't know what they were talking about. Then he remembered how Claire had looked when she had offered hope to Jonathan Fields's wife and how tears had filled his mother's eyes when she told him how she prayed for him, and his heart pricked.

They had something in their lives that he didn't have, and suddenly he wanted it, too. He took a deep breath and strode down the hall. Once inside his bedroom he went straight to the table beside the bed and rummaged through the drawer until he found what he wanted.

He hadn't seen it in years, not since he was a child, but he remembered the Christmas his grandmother had given it to him. He held the Bible in his hands and stared at it, not knowing where to open it. It had been so long, and he remembered very little about the words inside.

Then he smiled as a childhood memory of him reciting a verse for his family drifted into his head, and he opened it close to the middle and flipped through the pages until he found the chapter he was searching for.

He sat down on the side of the bed and began to read. "'The Lord is my shepherd; I shall not want.'"

TEN

Ever since she'd overheard Wes Stratton's conversation last night, she'd been unable to think of anything except that she and Adam finally had a lead on Peter Willis. If what he'd said was correct, Wes would arrive at Serenity sometime tomorrow. That gave her and Adam about twenty-four hours to scout out the place and determine if anything illegal was going on there.

She stared out the window as the car sped along the highway on their way to Serenity. This was her favorite time of year. The leaves on the trees that lined the four-lane road had changed from their summer green to the rich, bold colors of autumn. Soon they'd litter the ground, but for now they provided a perfect backdrop for the surrounding scenery.

Had Adam noticed the vibrant colors on the trees? He'd seemed lost in thought since they left Memphis, and she hadn't wanted to distract him from driving, but suddenly she could no longer stand the silence. She turned her head and stared at him.

"Aren't the leaves beautiful this year?"

His hand on the steering wheel jerked as if she'd startled him, and he darted a glance her way. "What did you say?"

"I asked if you'd noticed the leaves. I don't suppose you have, though. You haven't said two words since you picked me up after lunch. Is something wrong?"

He shook his head. "No. I'm just a bit preoccupied today."

"Is there a problem at the office?"

"No. I guess I'm just tired. I didn't get much sleep last night."

She frowned and stared at him. "Were you ill?"

"No. Just had a lot on my mind."

He didn't say anything else, and she turned to stare back out the window. Her mind raced as she thought back to how upset he'd been when he first found her by the Dumpster. Maybe he'd still been concerned about her impetuously following Wes Stratton.

She took a deep breath and swiveled in her seat. "Were you unable to sleep because you were angry with me?"

"No! What made you think I was angry with you?" He jerked his head around to stare at her, and for the first time Claire saw the red streaks in his eyes. She'd never seen him look so tired.

She shrugged. "Because I left the restaurant to follow Wes. I'm sorry I did that. I won't run off again without telling you where I'm going."

"Good," he said. "But that wasn't what kept me awake."

"Then what was it."

The muscle in his jaw flexed, and he inhaled. "If you must know, I was reading the Bible."

Her mouth dropped open in surprise. Of all the things

he might have said, that was the last one she would ever have suspected. "The Bible? But that's wonderful. What made you do that?"

He cocked an eyebrow and shook his head. "As if you don't know. All that talk about how much God loves me made me curious. I thought I'd see if I could find any answers to the questions I have."

A dim hope began to curl in the bottom of her heart. "And did you find them?" She could barely speak because her chest was so tight.

"I'm not sure. I only meant to read one chapter, but then I read another. And before I knew it, I'd read into the wee hours of the morning. It was like I couldn't get my fill." He glanced at her. "Does that make sense?"

"It does." She reached over and touched his arm. "You'll find your answers, Adam. I know you will. That's what I'm praying for."

"Thanks, Claire." She thought he was going to say more, but at that moment a sign signaling the turnoff for Serenity Wellness Center came into view. Adam pointed to it. "This is where we leave the main highway."

They drove for several miles down a paved road that was lined with towering trees and passed through the gated entrance to the center. As they pulled into the circle drive in front of the spa, Claire's mouth dropped open in awe. Whoever had designed and built this center must have wanted to impress customers before they ever entered the building.

The three-story white brick structure could have served as a plantation home in bygone years. With its six columns across the front porch and the two-story wings that jutted out on either side, it reminded Claire of a restored Louisiana plantation big house she'd visited with her parents when they'd been on vacation the summer she was twelve years old.

"What a beautiful building," she whispered as she stared, mesmerized by its beauty.

"Yeah," Adam said. "But remember outside appearances can be deceiving. We're here to find out what Serenity is really like on the inside. Are you ready for that?"

The question reminded her of why they had come to Serenity. According to Wes Stratton's conversation, Peter Willis would be here tomorrow. That meant this facility was connected in some way to a killer. Whether or not the staff here realized it still had to be determined. But she and Adam intended to find the answer before they left.

She nodded, took a deep breath and reached for the door handle. "To paraphrase your great-grandfather, it's time for Peter Willis to answer for the crimes laid against him."

Adam set their luggage down at the reception desk in the lobby of the wellness center and smiled at the young woman behind the counter. "I have reservations for two rooms. One in the name of Claire Walker and one for Adam Knight."

The clerk smiled and pulled some papers from a box in front of her. "Welcome to Serenity, Mr. Knight and Miss Walker. I hope you'll enjoy your stay with us and leave feeling rejuvenated and healthier than when you arrived."

Adam glanced over his shoulder and noticed that Claire had wandered over to a glass-enclosed case hanging on the wall and appeared engrossed in reading Serenity's services for their guests. He turned back to the woman at the counter. "Both my friend and I have had a lot of stress in our lives lately. I hope you're right about our stay."

"If you'd like, I'm sure Mr. Morrison, the director, would be happy to talk with you. He can help you both design the program you'd like to follow while you're here."

"That sounds great. Where can we find him?"

She scooted some papers toward him. "If you'll sign this and let me make a copy of the credit card you reserved the rooms with, I'll have one of our bellmen take your bags to your rooms. I'll get someone to show you to Mr. Morrison's office."

Adam slid his credit card across the counter and nodded. "I'd appreciate meeting him."

She focused her gaze on somebody across the lobby, and Adam glanced over his shoulder at the man entering the room from an office near the front door. She raised her hand and waved at him. "Mr. Holt, could I see you for a minute?"

From the muscular build to the dark suit to the short haircut, Adam had no trouble identifying this man as part of the security team at Serenity. He strode across the room and stopped at the front desk.

"Is there something I can do for you, Miss Edwards?"

She nodded toward Adam. "This is Mr. Knight. He and his friend Miss Walker would like to talk with Mr. Morrison. Would you show them to his office?"

The man turned to Adam and stuck out his hand. "I'm Bryce Holt, part of the security department here at Serenity. We're glad to have you as guests."

As Bryce extended his hand, his coat sleeve slipped

up and revealed a red-and-black tattoo of a spider-web that started at his wrist and spread up his arm. Adam tried to determine how far the design extended up Bryce's arm, but he couldn't because it was covered by his jacket. Adam pulled his gaze away from the colorful tattoo and shook the man's hand. "We're looking forward to our visit."

"Then follow me. I'll show you right to Mr. Morrison's office."

Adam motioned for Claire to join them, and they followed Bryce Holt down a hallway to the left of the lobby. The door to one of the offices about halfway down the hall stood open, and he led them into a room where a young woman sat behind a desk.

Bryce motioned for them to step up to the desk. "Hailey, these guests would like to speak with Mr. Morrison. Is he busy right now?"

She smiled. "He's never too busy to speak with a guest. Trudy's with him, but they should be about finished with their meeting."

She rose and opened a door that led into another office. "Mr. Morrison, I have some guests who would like to meet with you."

A male voice boomed from inside. "Show them in." Adam and Claire stepped around the secretary and into Brian Morrison's office. He came around his desk as they entered, his hand extended. "Welcome to Serenity."

Adam shook his hand. "Thanks for seeing us. I'm Adam Knight, and this is my friend Claire Walker."

He inclined his head in the direction of the young woman beside him. "This is Trudy Jacobsen. She's my right hand here at Serenity. She's the program director and oversees all of our activities. I don't know what I'd do without her."

Trudy laughed. "Mr. Morrison's just trying to make me feel good. He'd do quite well without me because he has made sure Serenity offers only the best services to its customers."

"That's good to hear," Claire said. "I'm looking forward to being pampered for a few days."

Mr. Morrison chuckled and indicated the two chairs in front of his desk. When they had taken their seats and Trudy had sat back down in her chair, he dropped down into his desk chair, propped his elbows on the chair arms and steepled his fingers.

"Now, what can I help you with today?"

Adam leaned forward in his chair. "We looked at your website, and we saw what is posted there. But I guess we just want to know more about what's involved in each of the classes and how we can schedule our time to get the most out of our visit."

Trudy spoke up. "I'll be the one who'll help you organize your stay. You let me know which activities you're most interested in, and I'll help get the maximum number of classes scheduled. All of our activities are designed to help you leave here feeling more energetic and stimulated. We offer spa treatments, which I think you'll really like, Miss Walker. There are exercise classes for both men and women, nutrition classes, massages and saunas."

Claire closed her eyes and sighed. "That sounds wonderful. I can hardly wait to start."

Adam looked at his watch and frowned. "It won't be long until dinnertime. I think both Claire and I could use a nap. Why don't we get started in the morning? I'd like to do one of the exercise classes for men."

"And I'd like to have a massage and maybe a manicure and pedicure," Claire said.

Trudy laughed and stood up. "I'll get you scheduled for that. Now go and rest for a while. Our chef is preparing a delicious dinner tonight. It's going to be a cool evening, but you might want to take a walk down to our lake."

"Where is that?" Adam asked.

Brian Morrison stood up. "Go out the front walk and take the path to your right. It leads down to the lake. It's well lit, and there are benches down there. It's many of our guests' favorite spot. Just remember to stay on the lit paths. Security patrols the grounds at night, but they'll know you're guests if you don't wander off the main trails."

"Thanks for letting us know," Adam said. "We'll remember that."

Brian Morrison smiled. "All our precautions are for the safety of our guests."

"I understand." Adam and Claire rose, and he took her by the arm. "A walk to the lake after dinner sounds like a plan, Claire. How about it?"

"I'd love to see the lake."

"Good. Then we'll check it out." They started toward the door, but Adam stopped and turned back to Brian Morrison. "There is one more thing."

"Oh, what's that?"

"What about the daytime? Does security patrol the grounds then, too? I've always been a hiker, and your website mentions that the back of your property borders the river. Is it all right to hike the forest trails and along the river?"

Brian and Trudy exchanged quick glances before he smiled. "That's not a good idea, Mr. Knight."

"Why not?"

"Because there are a lot of wild turkeys in the woods around here, and this is turkey-hunting season in Tennessee. Security does patrol, but of course they can't be everywhere at once. Sometimes hunters slip onto the property because they know the turkeys are here. They hunt with guns and with bow and arrows. It can be very dangerous if a person gets caught accidentally between a hunter and his prey. We caution our guests to stay close to the main building."

Adam nodded. "Oh, I see. Thanks for telling me."

Brian smiled again. "I just don't want to see you hurt, Mr. Knight."

Trudy cleared her throat, and Adam glanced around at her standing beside the open door, a clear signal their visit was over. "I'll be in the dining room at dinner," she said. "But in the meantime, if you need anything, let me know."

Adam smiled as he and Claire exited the room. "We will."

Once they were in the elevator, he glanced at Claire. "You were mighty quiet in there. What did you think?"

She pursed her lips and frowned. "I don't know. On the surface they seemed very open and friendly, but that excuse about turkey season didn't ring true with me."

"Me, neither. We may need to go in search of those turkeys ourselves."

The elevator stopped on their floor, and she laughed. Looping her arm through his, she pulled him off the elevator and into the hall. "I know you're about to fall asleep on your feet, but you still have a sense of humor. That's one of things I always liked about you."

He cocked an eyebrow and stared at her. "I thought you hated my attempts at making you and Jessica laugh when you two were younger."

"I did. Because it seemed you were always trying to make us feel like silly schoolgirls who didn't have a lick of sense in our heads." A teasing gleam lit her eyes, and his heart fluttered. "In case you haven't noticed, Mr. Knight, I am no longer a schoolgirl who can be intimidated. I'm a grown woman."

He watched as she walked down the hall to her room. She turned and waved at him before she disappeared inside. For a moment he thought he couldn't move, then he slowly walked to his own room across the hall from hers. Before he entered, he turned his head to stare at her closed door.

"You're wrong, Claire," he whispered. "I have noticed you're a grown woman."

ELEVEN

Claire couldn't believe how few guests there appeared to be at Serenity. She glanced around the empty dining room and whispered across the table to Adam. "No wonder we were able to get reservations so easily. There's hardly anyone here."

Adam folded his napkin and placed it next to his plate. "I've noticed there aren't many people around. In fact, I haven't seen anybody in the hall where we're staying. Maybe tomorrow will be busier."

Claire hadn't thought about not seeing anyone else in their hallway until now, and for some reason it frightened her. "Do you think we're the only people on that floor?"

"Could be."

An ominous queasiness curled in the pit of her stomach. "That seems strange."

Claire let her gaze drift over the room and came to a stop on the hostess station where their waiter and the woman who'd seated them appeared to be in deep conversation. The waiter said something, and they both looked at Claire.

Her uneasiness melted into something more like fright and spread through Claire. Her skin prickled at the thought that the two had been discussing her and Adam. The waiter picked up a small folder and walked toward their table.

When he arrived, he laid the leather folder beside Adam and smiled. "Your meals will be added to your final bill, but you have to charge it to your room."

Adam signed the paper inside, closed it and handed it back to the waiter. As he reached for it, the sleeve of his uniform slipped up and revealed the tattoo of a spiderweb on his arm. His face reddened, and he pulled his sleeve down to cover the tattoo.

Claire smiled up at him. "I wonder if you could tell me something," she said."

The waiter glanced from her to Adam. "If I can, ma'am."

"We were wondering why there are so few people here. Is it always this slow?"

He laughed and shook his head. "Oh, no. This just happens to be a slow night. We're booked solid for the next three days. Weekends are always like that. You were lucky you wanted a reservation on one of our lighter days."

Adam nodded. "I guess we were. But I'm surprised you get many guests at all with this place being so remote."

The waiter shook his head. "That seems to be one of the things our customers like best about Serenity. It's far from the hustle and bustle of the world. Being close to nature seems to help people relax."

Adam rubbed his stomach. "Well, it's helped me relax, and the food was outstanding. Give our regards to the chef."

"I'll do that, sir." He took a step back from the table

and smiled. "Thank you for dining with us tonight. I hope you enjoy the rest of your evening."

Claire waited until he had walked through the swinging doors into the kitchen before she leaned across the table and whispered to Adam. "What did you think about his explanation for so few people being here?"

"It sounded like something he'd rehearsed." Adam shrugged. "But who knows? He could be right about it being busier on weekends."

She lowered her voice. "Did you see that strange tattoo on our waiter's arm?"

"I did, but it's not the first one like it I've seen today."

"Where did you see it?"

"That guy from Security who took us to Brian Morrison's office."

"Really?" Claire leaned back in her chair and thought for a moment. "What are the chances of two people working for the same organization having such similar tattoos?"

Adam shrugged. "It depends. Maybe it's a coincidence, but then again it could have a hidden meaning."

Claire narrowed her eyes and stared at him, but he seemed to be having difficulty looking her in the eyes. After a moment he picked up his water glass and took a sip.

"You're not telling me something," she said.

Adam set the glass down and sighed. "It's just that I've spent a lot of time with fugitives who were hardened criminals, and I've encountered similar tattoos before."

She glanced over her shoulder to make sure no one was close enough to hear her. "Are you saying the tattoos could be connected?"

He nodded and crossed his arms on the table. "Yes.

Spiders catch prey in their webs, and from what I've learned, a tattoo of a spiderweb on a man's arm can mean he has served time in prison. The bigger the web, the more time behind bars."

Claire sat back in her seat. "Wow! I never knew that." After a moment she smiled. "I'm really getting an education on crime hanging out with you, Adam. Your world is a long way from my life as a librarian."

His jaw sagged, and he tilted his head to one side. "That's why I've tried to be there for you in the past few days. You stepped into something you didn't understand when you went after Peter Willis, and I don't want you to get hurt."

She reached out and covered his hand with hers. "Thank you, Adam. No one could have a better protector than you've been. Even though it's been rough at times, I'm glad we've had this time together."

He laced his fingers with hers and smiled. "Me, too. Now, how about that walk down to the lake? It's a little chilly tonight, but I think we'll make it okay."

"I'd like that."

They stood and walked out of the dining room and into the main lobby. They stopped at the front door, and Adam frowned slightly as he studied her. "Are you sure you're dressed warmly enough?"

She nodded. "I have a sweater on, and I wore my suede boots. They'll keep my feet warm, and the clog-style heels make it easy to walk."

"Clog style? What's that?"

Claire stifled a chuckle at the perplexed look on Adam's face. "The heels are chunky."

He shook his head and laughed. "Sorry. I don't know anything about women's fashions."

"Then maybe I'm not the only person learning something from our partnership. I'm helping with your education, too."

He nodded and opened the door for her. His eyes twinkled as he stared at her. "And I thank you for that, Miss Walker."

Claire arched an eyebrow and directed a teasing look at him as she started through the door. "It's a pleasure, Mr. Knight."

Before she stepped onto the porch, she glanced over her shoulder and saw their waiter in the hallway just outside the dining room talking on a cell phone. And he was staring straight at them. A surprised look flashed across his face when she spotted him. Then he muttered something into the phone, whirled around and strode back into the dining room.

A chill ran down Claire's spine at the man's reaction. Was he talking with someone about her and Adam? She shook the thought from her head and stepped through the front door.

Outside she walked to the top step and stopped. She turned her head slowly and stared back at the building.

"What's the matter?" Adam asked.

"We were being watched by our waiter when we left the dining room."

He looked back at the front door and nodded. "I wouldn't doubt it. I don't think we should trust anyone we've met here yet. I've found it always pays to be cautious."

"I'm sure you're right," Claire murmured.

He took her by the hand. "But let's not let our suspicions ruin this beautiful night. Come on. Let's walk down to the lake."

She nodded and started down the steps. As they turned onto the path that led to the lake, she glanced back at the center. The uneasiness she'd felt a few minutes ago returned. Adam was right. It was a beautiful night, but she couldn't help but think something evil lurked somewhere nearby at Serenity. And it was keeping them in its sights.

As they ambled along the path to the lake, Adam hoped he'd satisfied Claire's concerns about the possibility of their being watched. He didn't want her upset, but he still wanted her to be careful while they were at Serenity. So far he had no concrete proof that anyone was the wiser to why they were here, and he hoped to keep it that way.

Still, he had to admit that ever since they'd arrived he'd had a gut feeling they were only seeing what the staff at Serenity wanted them to see. For the protection of both of them, he had to stay on his game and not get distracted. And that was hard to do with Claire beside him on a clear, moonlit night.

They reached the lake at that moment, and Claire pointed to a bench near the water's edge. "Let's sit over there."

"All right."

He followed her to the spot, and they sank down on the bench. Neither spoke for a few minutes. Then Claire let out a long sigh. "Isn't the lake beautiful with the moonlight reflecting off the surface of the water?"

Adam nodded. "It is. I understand why they suggested we walk down here." He stretched out his legs and crossed his feet at the ankles. "I must say this is very peaceful."

Claire turned toward him. "It's good to see you relaxed. Ever since you found me at the cabin, your life has been filled with problems. I'm sorry I've disrupted everything for you."

He straightened, swiveled to face her and rested his arm on the back of the bench. "Don't think like that, Claire. I'm glad I could help you."

"I know you are, but if it wasn't for me, you wouldn't have been shot at or chased by a speeding car. And I don't want you put in any more danger because of me. Maybe I need to go back to Nashville and let the police find Peter Willis."

Her words shocked him, and he sat up straighter. "Go back? Why?"

"Because when I first started this, I didn't think about how it could affect other people. After the past few days, I've seen how my actions could have consequences for a lot of people."

His mouth dropped open, and he frowned. "What are you talking about, Claire?"

"I'm talking about your family. How could I ever face them again if something happened to you because you came with me on what I probably shouldn't have started in the first place?"

He didn't say anything for a moment, then he reached down and took her hand in his. "Claire, the job I do is dangerous. My family knows that. If anything happened to me, they wouldn't blame you."

The tears in the corner of her eyes glistened in the moonlight. "But I would blame myself." She took a deep breath. "Adam, now with both my parents gone, the closest thing I have to a family is yours. I don't want to hurt them."

Her words stirred a new hope in his heart. If she loved his family, then she might really have forgiven him for the things he had said to her in the past. Perhaps this could lead to a new relationship for the two of them.

He took a deep breath. "Are you saying that you love my family?"

"Of course I do. I practically grew up at your house. Your mom and dad have always treated me like I was one of the family. Nobody could feel any closer to a sister than I do to Jessica."

He dreaded asking the next question, but he had to know. "That leaves Lucas and me. What about us?"

She hesitated for a moment before she responded. "Any girl in her right mind would be happy to have two such fine men as brothers."

His heart dropped to the pit of his stomach. A brother. His chest felt so tight he could hardly breath.

She stared into his eyes, and a longing like he'd never known swept over him. He wanted to reach out and pull her into his arms. He wanted to tell her that he didn't want to be her brother. He wanted something more from her. He wanted to shout at her that he loved her, and he would give anything to erase the bad memories from her mind and make her love him.

But he knew it would do no good.

He struggled to smile and squeezed her hand. "Thank you for telling me this, Claire, but you haven't changed my mind about finding Peter Willis. I want to know what he is involved in that has cost the lives of four people. That we know of."

"But, Adam…" She frowned and tried to pull her hand away but he held on.

"No, Claire. You can go back to Nashville if you want, but I won't give up. I'm going to find him."

After a minute she nodded. "Okay, I'll stay until he's caught. But I'm not cut out to be a bounty hunter, and I don't want to run my dad's business. So as soon as this is all over, I'm going back to my job in Nashville."

Her words crushed him, but he nodded. "If that's what you want."

"It is."

He glanced up at the moon before he looked at her again. "It's getting late. Why don't we call it a night?"

"Okay."

They rose and headed back to the center in silence. They didn't speak or even glance at each other until they exited the elevator on their floor and stopped outside Claire's room. She pulled her key from her pocket and turned to Adam.

"Thank you for a lovely evening."

"I enjoyed it, too, Claire. What about in the morning? Want to meet for breakfast?"

She shook her head. "I don't think so. My spa appointment is set for 8:00 a.m., so I'll probably have them bring some coffee to my room before I go for that."

He nodded. "And I have that workout session about the same time. I'll check with you when I get back, though, and we can go to lunch."

"That sounds good."

Adam searched his mind for something else to say, but he could think of nothing. He pulled out his key and walked across the hall to his room. He glanced back over his shoulder before he stepped through the door. Claire was still standing outside her room, a strange expression on her face.

He gave a feeble smile. "Good night, Claire."

"Good night, Adam."

The door closed, and he stood in his room rethinking the things Claire had said when they were at the lake. The only conclusions he could draw was that she had found a way to let him know there was no chance for the two of them to have a relationship. She thought of him as a brother, just as she did his brother, Lucas.

A brother? The thought sent anger surging through him. He didn't want to be her brother. Couldn't she tell he loved her? Apparently she did, and she had tried to let him down in a nice way tonight. But it hadn't worked. He would never be okay with her not loving him back.

He stormed across the room, sat down on the edge of the bed and gripped the sides of the mattress with his hands. A week ago he'd been content to go about his work every day and not let thoughts of a woman interfere with his life. That all had changed the night he charged out of the Mississippi woods and found Claire lying on the ground.

Now he didn't think he would ever be able to return to what he'd known before that, and the thought made him sadder than anything ever had.

TWELVE

Claire watched as Adam walked into his room and closed the door behind him. A tear ran down the side of her face, and she wiped it away with her hand. Their conversation at the lake had left her confused. What did he want from her?

She'd told herself dozens of times over the past few years that she was better off without Adam. He'd broken her heart once, and he didn't share her belief in God. Those were two strikes against him, but it didn't seem to matter. She knew she'd always love him in spite of those things.

Tonight when she'd brought up the possibility of returning to Nashville, she had hoped he would take her in his arms and beg her to stay. But he didn't. He sat there as if he was made of the same stone that the bench was and listened to her ramble on about how she loved his family and didn't want them to blame her if he was hurt.

She had voiced her confession because she hoped that if she told him how she felt about his family, he would assure her that they all loved her, too, just like he did. But that had never happened.

His reaction had been aloof and left her wondering

if it had made him angry. Perhaps he wanted her to realize that even though they had buried their differences
over what had happened between them six years ago, she
wasn't a part of his family and never would be.

If that's the way he felt, then she needed to get back to
Nashville as soon as possible. As soon as they returned
to Memphis, she'd close her father's business and put
his house up for sale. Then she'd go back to the dull life
she'd lived for the past few years.

More tears filled her eyes as she slid her key in the
door and pushed it open. She glanced over her shoulder
once more at Adam's door before she sighed and walked
into the darkened room.

The door clicked shut behind her, and she flipped the
light switch on the wall. As the overhead light blinked
on, she froze at the sound of movement behind her. Before she could turn around, an arm wrapped around her
neck and another encircled her waist. She opened her
mouth to scream, but the pressure on her neck increased
and a man's voice whispered in her ear.

"Don't move, Miss Walker, or I'll kill you."

Panic swept through her, and she stilled. She wanted
to speak, to ask him what he wanted with her, but the
only sound she could make was a gasp as she struggled
to breathe.

He pressed his cheek to hers, and she realized he
wore a wool ski mask. She trembled at the touch of his
face next to hers, but she tried not to move. "That's better," he whispered. "Now just relax. This will be over
in a few minutes."

She opened her mouth and gulped a big breath of air.
"Wh-what are you going to do?"

He chuckled and pulled his arm tighter around her

neck. "You should never have come to Serenity, Miss Walker. Now you have to disappear."

"You can't get away with this," she gasped. "Adam will tell the police."

He chuckled. "I don't think so. There are plans to make him disappear, too. In fact, there's nothing to prove that you were ever here at all."

His arm tightened around her neck, and she pressed back against him. She was about to lose consciousness, and she couldn't let that happen. Instinct kicked in, and she grabbed the hand around her throat with both of hers as she turned her head into his shoulder. Then with all the strength she could muster, she raised her hands over her head and pounded at his face.

The man howled in pain and released the pressure on her neck. His arm still circled her waist, but she wriggled in his hold and struck at him again. Once free from his hold, she whirled around and lunged at him, her curled fingers scratching and gouging at his eyes while she screamed at the top of her lungs.

He staggered backward and crossed his arms in front of his face to ward off her attack. Claire's eyes widened as the sleeve of his black sweatshirt slipped up to reveal a black-and-red spiderweb tattooed on his arm.

She only got a glimpse of the tattoo before he recovered from her surprise attack and lunged back toward her. Claire screamed and grabbed the straight-backed chair sitting at the room's desk and hurled it at him as he pulled a gun from a holster attached to the waistband of his jeans and aimed at her.

The chair crashed against his arm and knocked the gun from his hand. It hit the floor between them, and they both dove for it. Claire's fingers grazed the metal of the pistol before he whisked it from her hand. A new fear overtook her as she gazed into the barrel of the gun pointed at her head.

She swallowed and closed her eyes just as the door crashed open.

"Drop the gun or you're a dead man!"

The man whirled away from her toward the voice coming from the door. Claire opened her eyes to see Adam standing there, his gun pointed at the man in the mask. The man pointed his gun at Claire's head. "I'm having trouble controlling my finger. You sure would hate for me to shoot your girlfriend, wouldn't you?"

Adam took another step into the room. "Get away from her."

The man chuckled, reached down and hauled Claire to her feet. He clamped his arm around her chest, pinning her arms to her sides, and raised the gun to her head. "Back off now, Knight, or I'll kill her." He turned his mouth to her ear and whispered, "Don't try any of your tricks this time, or I'll shoot him."

Claire stared at Adam, unable to speak, but he appeared locked in a battle of wills with the man holding her hostage. He exhaled and crept forward another step. "I told you to let her go."

The man tightened his hold on her and laughed. "It looks like we have a standoff here. I tell you what I'm going to do. I'll start counting. By the time I get to three if you haven't laid your gun down, I'll blow her head off."

Adam's hand gave a slight wobble, but he didn't put the gun down.

"One," the man said. "You better believe me, Knight."

Adam didn't move.

"Two." He paused a moment. "Are you really willing for her to be killed?"

Adam didn't reply, and the man shook his head. "I'm not bluffing. I'll do it."

Adam still made no reply but kept his gun trained on his target.

"Have it your way. Thr—"

Adam's gun clattered to the floor, and he raised his hands. "I put it down. Now let her go."

The man lowered the gun and waved it in Adam's direction. "Move out of the way."

"You're not leaving here with her."

"Oh, yes, I am. If you try anything, I'll shoot you first and then finish what I started before you burst in here. Now move out of my way."

Adam glanced at his gun on the floor and back at her. "Claire, I'm not going to let him hurt you."

"It's all right, Adam. Move before he shoots you."

The man pushed the gun harder against her temple. "Get out of the way!"

Adam moved aside as her captor nudged Claire toward the door. She lifted her foot as if to take a step but instead raised it higher and smashed the chunky heel of her boot straight down onto the top of his foot.

He squealed in pain and jerked backward. Before he could recover, she rammed her heel down again and pressed it into his foot with all her weight. Out of the corner of her eye she saw Adam lunge for his gun. Then he grabbed her and spun her behind him.

The masked intruder raised his gun, but Adam fired first. The man jerked as the bullet plowed into his shoulder. Then her assailant fired off three quick rounds that sprayed the room as he ran toward the door.

He disappeared into the hall, and Adam turned to Claire. "Are you all right?"

Her teeth chattered so hard that all she could do was nod.

He grabbed her by both shoulders and stared into her eyes. "I'm going after this guy. Stay here until I get back. Understand?"

She wanted to speak. To beg him not to leave her alone. But she knew it would be useless. He needed to catch this person who had tried to kill them.

She cleared her throat and nodded. "Go."

His gaze raked her face once more before he ran to the door and disappeared into the hall. She could hear the tap of his running footsteps as he rushed toward the stairway exit. There were no other sounds. No other guests running from their rooms to inquire about shots being fired. No spa security officers rushing up the stairs to investigate.

What was going on in this place?

After a moment she heard footsteps and tensed. She held her breath until Adam appeared in the doorway. "What happened?" she asked.

Adam didn't take his eyes off her as he walked into the room. "There was a car waiting for him. They drove off just as I got outside."

The fear she'd tried to ignore returned, and she began to shake. She wrapped her arms around her waist as tears rolled down her face. "H-he w-was waiting for me when I came into the room. I didn't see him until he grabbed me." The last words dissolved into a sob.

Adam stood still for a moment, and then he reached out as if he was offering an invitation she could either accept or refuse. There was only one place she wanted to be right now. She stared up into his eyes and with a moan threw herself against him. He wrapped his arms around her and pulled her close as she sobbed.

"It's okay, Claire," he crooned. "It's over now, and we're all right."

Her arms crept around him, and she pressed her face against his chest. She could hear his heart beating, and the sound comforted her. She closed her eyes and said a silent prayer of thanks to God for bringing them through this attack safely and asked Him to protect them in the future. Something told her that whoever wanted her dead wouldn't stop because of their failure tonight.

They'd try it again, and she and Adam were going to have to be on high alert if they were to survive the next time.

Adam tightened his arms around Claire and pressed his cheek to the top of her head. The fruity scent of her shampoo filled his nostrils, and he inhaled deeply. Although he realized her need for him at the moment was sparked by her fear at almost being killed, holding her like this seemed so right.

He waited for her to calm down before he said anything. "Claire, I think we need to go."

She jerked her head back and stared up at him. "Go?"

He nodded. "Yes. Don't you think it's strange no one has come to investigate? There were shots fired in this room. You'd think someone would have heard."

"I wondered about that. Where should we go?"

"Somewhere safe for the night so we can figure out what our next step is. Get whatever you brought, and let's leave."

"Okay."

She pulled away from him, rushed to the closet and pulled out her suitcase. With his gun in his hand, he walked back to the door and stood watch while she packed. Nobody entered the hallway from either end.

"I'm ready," she said.

She stopped beside him, her suitcase in hand. "What about your clothes?"

"I keep my bag packed when I'm on a job. Never can tell when I'm going to have to leave a place in a hurry. I'll get it."

He scanned the hallway in both directions before he stepped out and motioned for her to follow. Quickly he unlocked his door and grabbed his suitcase, which sat just inside the room. Then, nodding toward the exit stairs at the end of the hallway, he headed toward them with her right behind.

Once they were outside the building, they circled around to the front parking lot where he'd left his car. A few minutes later they were driving down the road that led to the main highway. When they reached it, Adam turned left instead of turning right toward Memphis.

"Where are we going?" Claire asked.

"I want to find a safe place for the night. They will probably look for us in Memphis. So I don't want us to go home."

"Do you have any ideas about where we'll stay?"

"Do you remember my aunt Sue, my mother's sister?"

Claire nodded. "Yes, Jessica and I used to spend a week with her every summer."

"She lives about thirty miles from here. She'll put us up for the night. In the morning we can decide what to do next."

"That sounds good."

She settled back in her seat and closed her eyes. Within a few minutes a soft snore drifted through the car. Adam smiled and checked the heater to make sure it was turned high enough and then directed his attention to the road ahead.

As he drove through the night, he glanced at her sleeping form from time to time. The thought of what had almost happened tonight made his stomach queasy, and he swallowed. What if he hadn't heard her scream? She'd be dead by now. He thought back to what he'd told her about deciding what to do in the morning. What he hadn't told her was that he already knew what to do.

He didn't know anyone else who could have coped so well with all the danger she'd faced in the past few days. His lips twitched at the thought of her boot heel grinding into her attacker's foot. It was as if she had a natural-born instinct for how to defend herself, but that didn't mean he was going to put her in danger again.

He'd finalized his plan as he'd driven toward his aunt's house, and he knew the perfect way to keep her safe. Tomorrow morning he would return to Serenity and try to find out what secrets were being covered up there, but Claire wasn't going along. He'd slip away and leave her at his aunt's house.

He could only imagine how angry she'd be when she discovered that he'd left without her, but he had to do it. Maybe later she'd come to realize he'd done it for her own good. Or better yet, that he'd kept her safe because he didn't want to see the woman he loved hurt.

He tightened his grip on the steering wheel and gritted his teeth. By this time tomorrow night he suspected he would either know Peter Willis's connection to Serenity and whatever was going on there, or he'd be dead.

The same fear he'd felt before going into battle curled in his stomach, and he groaned. When he'd been in the military, he'd been part of a squad. Tomorrow he'd be alone. Could he do it?

Next to him Claire mumbled in her sleep, and the sound soothed him. Over the past few days, he'd come to know a part of her that he hadn't before. Not only was she beautiful and a bit willful at times, but she was strong and courageous, unafraid to fight back when an attacker was holding a gun to her head. It had to take a deep faith in God to do that.

He remembered one of the Bible verses he'd read last night about how God was with you when you walked through the valley of the shadow of death. They had walked that path tonight, and they'd lived. He was beginning to believe she'd been right all along, and he'd been wrong.

He stared through the windshield up at the stars and said a silent prayer of thanks to God for sparing their lives tonight. *And, God,* he prayed, *help me find the answers that will bring closure for Claire over the loss of her father.*

Peace flowed through him, and he smiled. There was no doubt in his mind that God would be watching out for him tomorrow. His years of training had prepared him for what he must do. He just needed to be alert for dangers around him and be ready to deal with whatever came his way. And most of all he would need to put the outcome in God's hands.

THIRTEEN

Claire couldn't believe she'd dropped off to sleep the minute her head hit the pillow and had slept so soundly last night. She sat on the side of the bed while she pulled her boots on and glanced around the bedroom where she and Jessica had spent so many happy times together.

She'd always enjoyed coming here, and last night it had seemed like a safe haven when Adam had led her inside. She barely remembered her conversation with his aunt other than to thank her, but she felt safe among people she loved.

She stood up, smoothed the bedspread back in place and headed toward the kitchen. The smell of fresh coffee drifted through the house, and her stomach rumbled with hunger. At the kitchen door she paused and studied Adam, who sat at the table while he read the morning newspaper.

He didn't see her, and she took the opportunity to drink in his handsome features. His dark hair, still wet from the shower, curled a bit at the back, and a day's growth of beard shadowed his face. His dark eyes stared at the printed page in front of him.

She cleared her throat and smiled when he looked up. "Good morning."

A surprised look flashed across his face. "I didn't expect you up so early. After all that happened last night, I thought you'd sleep later."

"No, I feel great. Slept like a log."

He pointed to the counter where the coffeepot sat. "There's coffee, and Aunt Sue made some muffins this morning."

"Um, that sounds good." After pouring herself a cup of coffee and picking up a muffin, she sat down at the table and looked around. "Where is Aunt Sue?"

"She left for work a few minutes ago. She said she'd see you later today."

Claire frowned as she swallowed a bite of muffin and glanced at Adam. "Later today? Are we coming back here when we leave Serenity?"

He tightened his hold on his cup and twirled it in small circles as he stared down into the coffee inside. "We'll see what happens."

"I'm ready to go anytime you are. I thought we might be outdoors most of the day, so I put on some comfortable clothes, and I brought my heavy jacket when I came downstairs." She pointed to her boots. "And I'm wearing my boots that came in so handy last night in case we run into another one of our stalkers."

He stared down at her boots for a moment before he lifted his gaze and looked into her eyes. "I'm sorry about last night, Claire. I should never have let that guy get so close to you."

The stricken look in his eyes pierced her heart, and she reached across the table to him. He laced his fingers with hers and squeezed. "Adam, you can't blame yourself for what happened. There's no way you could have prevented it."

"Yes, I could have. I should have gone into your room first and checked it out instead of leaving you alone in the hallway. For a moment I forgot what I was doing there."

She frowned. "I don't understand what you're saying."

He raked his hand through his hair and sighed. "Instead of concentrating on the danger around us I got too caught up in the moon and how beautiful you looked. All I could do was think about six years ago, and I let my regrets get in the way of my job to protect you."

His words shocked her. She had to make him understand that what happened wasn't his fault. "Adam, you can't take responsibility for someone else's actions. That guy was waiting for me, and he might have killed you if you had gone into the room first. I could have asked you to check out my room, but I didn't. My independent streak wouldn't let me admit I might need some help." She grinned at him. "But when I needed you, you came running. Even kicked the door in."

He chuckled. "Yeah, I did. And my leg's a bit sore today from doing it."

She let go of his hand and straightened in her chair. "Then you need to take it easy until we get ready to leave for Serenity."

His face flushed, and he glanced at his watch. "Wow! I didn't realize it was getting so late. I need to call the office and see if Jessica made it back from Louisiana okay." He pulled his cell phone from his pocket. "And I need to get some things upstairs. So I'll make the call from there. Enjoy your breakfast."

"Tell Jessica I said hi," she called after him. He was out of the room before she could finish her sentence.

Claire took another bite and washed it down with a swig of coffee. Adam had surprised her this morning with his talk about feeling responsible for her almost being killed. She hoped she had relieved his mind some.

She started to take another sip of coffee but stopped and frowned. Come to think of it, he had acted nervous and ill at ease from the moment she walked into the kitchen. After a moment she shrugged. He probably had a lot on his mind about what they were going to do at Serenity today.

She opened her mouth to take another bite of her muffin but stopped before she bit into it. *Wait just a minute,* she thought. He'd been very vague about the trip to Serenity today. In fact, it was almost as if he was avoiding answering her questions.

The conversation they'd had replayed in her mind, and she mulled over his guilt about her attack. Then his speedy retreat to make a phone call. Suddenly her eyes widened as she remembered he'd said Aunt Sue would see her later today. When she'd asked him if they were returning, he had dismissed it with a "we'll see what happens" answer.

The truth hit her, and her mouth dropped open. He had left her eating her breakfast while he made his preparations to slip away without her. That's why Aunt Sue would see *her* later. Because Adam had decided Claire wasn't going anywhere.

She jumped up from her chair, stormed out of the kitchen and headed to the staircase. She could hear Adam's voice upstairs as he talked on the phone, and she stopped. No, she wouldn't confront him about his plan to leave her behind. Two could play at this game.

She hurried into the den, clicked the TV on and turned the volume up loud enough to be heard in the hallway. Then she rushed back to the coat rack by the door where she'd left her jacket when she came down earlier and closed the door quietly as she exited the house.

His car sat in the driveway where he'd parked it last night, and she ran toward it. She glanced over her shoulder, but Adam was nowhere in sight yet. Smiling, she opened the door and lay down in the backseat to wait for Adam.

He was in for quite a surprise when he came outside.

Adam finished his phone call to his office, shrugged into his coat and crept down the stairs. He could hear one of the early-morning news shows playing on the TV as he stepped into the hall, and he smiled. Good. Claire was watching TV and wouldn't hear him leave.

The door clicked closed as he slipped from the house, and he headed to his car. He climbed in and chuckled as he pulled out of the driveway. He'd gotten away without her being any the wiser. He only hoped she wouldn't be too angry when she discovered he'd left without her. If things went well today, he'd have the chance to explain his reasons to her. Maybe she'd forgive him then.

He was still laughing to himself a mile later when he stopped at a red light. He glanced out the window at the parking lot of a convenience store to his left and then to his rearview mirror. The scowling face reflecting back at him made his heart slam into his chest.

"What are you…?" he muttered as he swiveled in his seat to get a better look at Claire.

"Doing here?" she finished for him. He blinked in case he was only imagining that she sat in the backseat, her arms crossed, and an angry expression wrinkling her face.

The car behind them honked, and Claire pointed to the traffic light. "The light's turned green. You're holding up traffic."

"Claire!" Her name exploded from his mouth, and he jerked his body around to face forward. He pressed the accelerator, and the car lurched forward.

Still muttering under his breath, he pulled into the turn lane at the entrance to a large retail store and pulled to a stop in their parking lot. Before he could turn off the ignition, Claire had climbed into the passenger seat beside him. She leaned over so close to him that their noses almost touched.

"Before you start yelling at me, I want you to know that your little act didn't fool me one bit. How could you try to run off from me like that? I thought we were in this together."

He glanced around to see if her shrill words had attracted any attention, but no one seemed to be paying them any mind. He took a breath to yell back at her, but the hurt look in her eyes made him pause.

He exhaled and sank back in his seat. "I care about what happens to you, and I only wanted to protect you, Claire. These guys have tried to kill you four times now. I don't want their fifth attempt to be successful. I did what I thought was best for you."

The anger disappeared from her face. "I appreciate your wanting to protect me, but I don't want you in danger, either. If I hadn't been so headstrong and started all this by myself, Peter Willis might have been caught by now. I have to see this finished, and we need to do this together."

He shook his head. "No, I'm taking you back to Aunt Sue's house. Wait there for me."

"And what if you never come back? What am I supposed to do?"

He forced a laugh. "Don't talk like that. Of course I'll come back. The bounty hunters of the Knight Agency always get their man."

A small smile pulled at her mouth. "This time the bounty hunter has an assistant who isn't taking no for an answer. I'm going with you. If you try to leave me behind, I'll get a car and follow you."

She crossed her arms and directed a stern glare in his direction. After a moment he shook his head and laughed. "Okay, Claire. Against my better judgment, we'll go together. But you have to promise that you'll do as I say."

She tilted her head to one side. "You know that I've never been very good at following orders."

He sucked in his breath and leaned toward her. "Claire, you are the most infuriating woman I have ever met."

She laughed, reached up and patted his cheek. "Just joking, Adam. For today I'll try to let you be the boss."

A warm rush poured through him at the touch of her hand and the teasing glint in her eyes. He swallowed in an effort to relieve the pressure in his chest, then reached over and turned the ignition.

The motor purred to life, and he smiled at her. "Then let's go get the bad guys."

Claire had kept up a steady stream of chatter ever since they left the parking lot and headed down the highway in the direction of Serenity. He tried to listen, but his mind kept wandering to the question of what they were going to do once they arrived at the spa. They couldn't walk in the front door and demand to know what kind of secrets the center was hiding. "Do you agree with that?" Claire asked.

Adam realized Claire had just said something, but he didn't have any idea what it was. He glanced at her. "Huh?"

"I said don't you agree with me?"

"Oh, sure. Anything you say." She didn't respond for a moment, and he darted a glance at her. Her eyebrows were drawn across her nose in a big frown, and she glared at him. "What's the matter?" he said.

She released a big huff of breath and shook her head. "Men! They don't ever listen to women."

"I was listening. You asked if I agreed, and I said I did."

"So you'd really like to see me dye my hair bright orange and have my nose pierced with a ring?"

The steering wheel jerked in his hands as he cast a startled look at her. "Are you serious?"

She rolled her eyes and exhaled. "Of course not. But you weren't listening to me, and I thought I'd see what it took to get your attention."

He chuckled and directed his attention back to the road. "You've got it now. I vote 'no' on the hair and piercing."

She smiled. "Good." She was quiet for a moment. "What were you so lost in thought about?"

"Trying to decide what our first move should be."

"And have you found the answer yet?"

He nodded. "I think so." At that moment he spotted a gravel road in the distance off to the right of the main highway. He pointed to it. "See that road? It's about a mile from there to where you turn off to go to Serenity. I think we need to go down that road until we get to the river, then hike over to Serenity's property, and see what we can discover."

"That sounds good to me."

He turned on the road and drove about a mile until he came to a dead end. He drove into a clearing atop a small bluff and parked the car. "We'll leave the car here and follow the river to the center."

They climbed out and looked around at the littered area. Soft drink cans, candy wrappers and potato chip containers were scattered around the clearing. "This must be a hangout for teenagers wanting to party," Claire said.

"Yeah. Lucky for us they should all be in school today." Adam frowned as he looked at the thick forest growth just beyond the clearing. "This doesn't look like it's going to be an easy hike. Are you up to this?"

"I will be in a minute," she said as she opened the back door of the car and reached inside.

His eyes grew wide when she straightened, and he saw her holding a gun and holster. "What are you doing with that?"

"Making sure I'm armed." She buckled the holster around her waist and checked to make sure it was secure.

He shook his head. "No way am I going to let you carry that. You aren't experienced enough."

"I won't draw it unless it's a matter of life or death. Now let's go."

She started to take a step, but he grabbed her arm. He stared down at her. "I thought you were going to let me be the boss today."

She pulled her arm free and smiled. "I said I'd *try* to let you be the boss. Now let's go."

"I never had this much trouble with Lucas or Jessica when we were working on a case together. I don't know what I did to deserve you."

She batted her eyelashes at him. "Just lucky, I guess. Now are you coming with me?"

He stared at her and shook his head as she turned and walked toward the forest. After a moment he followed her along the river on their way to Serenity.

It was time to find out the truth.

FOURTEEN

Claire hadn't realized how difficult it would be to maneuver through the forest that ran along the river. Twice she tripped over exposed tree roots and landed on the ground. Both times Adam pulled her to her feet, and she trudged on as if nothing had happened.

It took them nearly an hour to make the one-mile trek through the woods, and she was out of breath by the time they reached a wire fence with a sign hanging on it that stated this was private property of the Serenity Wellness Center, and trespassers would be prosecuted.

She stopped and eyed the fence. "That's not an electric fence, is it?"

Adam pulled a pair of leather gloves out of his pocket and slipped them on his hands. "No. It's barbed wire. Be careful. It can make a mean cut."

He put both his gloved hands on the top strand and pushed down with all his weight until the wire dipped low. "Step over it while I'm holding it down."

Claire raised one leg and stepped over, then did the same with the other. She almost had her foot on the ground when she heard a rip and glanced down to see a long tear in her jacket.

She shook her head in disgust and made her way over the fence.

When Adam was safely over the wire, they continued their hike in the direction of the spa. The trail became steeper, and the tree line skirted the top of the bluff. Adam stopped and studied the dirt path that continued along the bluff.

"This trail is getting narrower. It may run out before long. We need to climb up the bluff and into the trees. The leaves haven't fallen yet, so we'll have more cover there than we do on this exposed path."

He took hold of her arm and guided her up the steep bank and into the forest. They continued in the same direction but stopped suddenly at the sound of voices drifting on the air. Claire turned to Adam, but he put his finger over his lips to silence her. As they crept forward through the trees, the voices grew louder, but it was still difficult to make out the words.

Trying not to make a sound, they crept through the trees until they arrived at the edge of a clearing. A large barn, painted bright red and with a metal roof like so many other barns in the rural area, occupied the middle of the open space. Three white service vans and several cars sat near the tall front double doors.

Adam dropped to the ground and pulled Claire down next to him. She turned to him and whispered, "What do you think they're doing?"

"I don't know, but we can't let them see us."

The front doors of the building opened, and two men walked outside. Their voices carried on the wind, and Claire strained to hear what they were saying.

"The boss is bringing in a lot of food for tonight.

He must have some big deals in the works," one of the men said.

The other one laughed, picked up a box from the van and handed it to the first man before he grabbed another one. "I heard this is the biggest night ever."

"Have they found those two bounty hunters who got away last night?"

"I haven't heard. But then people have a way of disappearing around here, and you never know what happened to them."

His friend laughed. "You got that right."

They disappeared back into the building, and Claire turned to Adam. "They're taking food into a barn for the guests who are coming tonight? What do you think is going on here?"

"I don't know, but from what they said, they haven't given up trying to find us."

The roar of a car caught their attention, and they watched as a black SUV stopped in front of the building. The driver turned off the motor and opened the door. Claire clamped her hand over her mouth to keep from making a sound when Wes Stratton stepped from the car. With his Western jacket, cowboy boots and Stetson hat, he looked as if he'd just driven in from Texas instead of Memphis.

The front door of the barn opened, and Claire pressed her hand tighter against her lips when Peter Willis stepped outside. Their dining room waiter from the night before followed him and stopped behind him. They both stared at Wes before Peter spoke. "Wes, it's good to see you."

A scowl covered Wes's face. "I told you I'd be here today. And I am."

"I never doubted you for a moment," Peter said. "Do you have something for me?"

Wes nodded, reached back in the vehicle and pulled a black bag out. "I did the best I could, but I only have half of it. It was impossible to get my hands on that much money in such a short amount of time. I'll get it for you, though."

Peter's expression didn't change. "Wes, you disappoint me."

Wes took off his hat and rubbed his forehead with a handkerchief he pulled from his pocket. "Listen, Peter, I'm good for it. All I need is a little more time."

"I've already given you more time, and look what you've done. Shown up here with only half of what you owe. You know how the boss feels about that."

Wes nodded. "I know. I know. But you'll get it. Just a few more weeks is all I need."

Peter cocked his head to one side and studied Wes for a moment. "A few more weeks, huh? I don't think the boss will go for that, but you never know." He glanced over his shoulder to the waiter. "Louis, get Mr. Stratton's bag."

Louis walked over to Wes and took the bag from him. Then he stepped behind him.

Wes cast a worried glance over his shoulder at Louis, but Peter smiled and motioned for him. "Come on in, Wes, and let's see what you have."

Wes had only taken two steps when Louis pulled out a gun and shot him in the back. Horrified, Claire rammed her fist in her mouth to muffle her cries and watched as Wes Stratton's lifeless body slumped to the ground.

Peter put his hands in his pockets and walked back to where Wes lay and took the bag from Louis. "Too bad," he said. "I liked Wes, but you can't hold out on the boss and live to talk about it."

"What do you want me to do now?" Louis asked.

"Get somebody to clean up this mess before the guests arrive, and then get rid of the body. You know where. Have somebody take his SUV over to that chop shop we use and then get back here to help us get ready for tonight."

"Yes, sir."

Claire felt a tug on her arm, and she glanced around at Adam. He motioned for her to follow him back through the trees. They slipped silently back toward the river and retraced their steps to the barbed-wire fence.

When they had climbed over and were once again in the forest next to Serenity's property, Claire grabbed Adam by the arm. "I have to stop for a minute."

She sank to the ground, and he sat down next to her. "I was right not to want you to come today. You shouldn't have seen that."

Tears ran down her face. "They killed him, Adam. Without giving it a thought. It was like he didn't matter. What kind of animals are these people?"

"They're vicious, Claire, and I don't want you near them again."

"What are we going to do? We can't let them get away with this."

"We have to go to the police, and we need to do it now. Can you make it back to the car?"

She rose to her feet. "I can. Let's go."

They hurried through the forest as fast as they dared go with all the exposed roots and vegetation covering the ground, but the trip back seemed to take longer than it had on their way over. Claire gasped for breath, but she fought the urge to beg Adam to stop for another short rest. They had to get out of there as quickly as possible.

After what seemed an eternity, she saw the edge of the forest and the clearing beyond where they'd parked the car. "Just a few more feet, Claire, and we'll be there," Adam called out.

They burst out of the forest but stopped in horror at what confronted them. An SUV with its motor idling sat next to Adam's car and Peter Willis, with his arms crossed and grinning as if he'd just pulled off the biggest joke of his life, leaned against the fender of Adam's car.

Claire skidded to a stop as Adam put his left arm out and shoved her behind him. With his right he pulled his gun from its holster and aimed it at Peter. Peter smiled and straightened to his full height. "I've been waiting for you. What took you so long?"

"That's close enough, Willis. Now put your hands up. There's a warrant for your arrest, and I'm here to serve it," Adam snarled.

Peter chuckled and took a step toward them. "I wouldn't be too sure about that." He looked past Adam and Claire and smiled. "Be careful of her boots. I hear they can do a lot of damage."

Adam grasped the gun tighter. "What are you talking about?"

"Why don't you take a look over your shoulder?"

As Adam turned to look at her, Claire felt her gun being pulled from its holster and something being pressed against the back of her head. She turned her head slightly to see over her shoulder. She slumped against Adam at the sight of Louis with her pistol in one hand and the other holding a gun to her head.

Adam's eyes narrowed as he studied Peter, but he

didn't lower his gun. Brian Morrison's words about the woods being patrolled flashed in Claire's mind, and she wondered how long Peter had known they were watching the activity at the building where Wes Stratton had been killed.

Now how were they going to get out of this mess?

Adam glanced from Louis to Peter as if he were trying to choose his best course of action. Before he could act, the door of the car next to his opened, and Bryce Holt stepped out. The gun he held was pointed straight at Adam.

Peter's face hardened into an angry mask. "Drop the gun now, or your lady friend is going to be sorry."

The tone of Peter's voice left little doubt that he would follow through with his threat. Adam glanced over his shoulder at Claire once more before he dropped his gun to the ground. "Okay, Willis, I've done what you asked. Now let Claire go."

Peter looked at Bryce and chuckled. "Can you believe this guy? After all the problems they've caused us he expects me to let her waltz out of here and go straight to the police. Put them in the car, and let's get out of here."

Bryce nodded and hobbled forward. When he reached Adam, he bent down, picked up Adam's gun and slipped it in his coat pocket. Then he grabbed Claire by the hair and pulled until she stood on tiptoes staring up into his eyes.

Her scream echoed through the silent forest, and Adam drew back to hit Bryce. Before he could, Louis pressed the barrel of his gun against Adam's back. "Take it easy unless you want to die right here."

Bryce gave a low chuckle, glared at Claire and shoved

her against Adam. "You're going to pay for breaking my foot last night, and I'm going to enjoy watching."

Adam put his arms around Claire, and she buried her face in his chest. Her body trembled, and she gasped for breath. He hugged her closer. "Leave her alone. You deserved everything you got last night. Only a coward attacks a woman like you did Claire. I hope every time you feel a pain in that foot you remember the woman who got the best of you."

Bryce's face turned red with anger, and he raised his gun. Before he could act, Peter stepped forward. "We're wasting time here. Louis, get that rope out of the car and tie them up so we can go. Then I want you to get rid of their car and meet us back at the barn."

Bryce jerked Claire out of Adam's arms and pulled her toward the car. "I'll take the girl, Louis. You take care of Knight."

Claire's heart pounded as thoughts of how they were going to get out of this predicament raced through her head. At the moment it seemed impossible, but there had to be something they could do. For the time being, they needed to stay alert and watch for Peter and his henchmen to make any kind of mistake that they could take advantage of.

She hoped it came soon, because right now their prospects for survival were looking very slim.

Claire and Adam, their hands tied behind their backs, sat side by side in the rear seats of the SUV as Bryce drove it away from the clearing. She glanced at Adam, and he leaned closer to whisper in her ear.

"Don't worry. We're going to get out of this."

The look on her face told him that his words, spoken

to give her some encouragement, hadn't really worked. She swallowed and nodded. "We'll think of something."

Peter, who sat in the front seat beside Bryce, turned in his seat and frowned at them. "What are you two whispering about back there?"

"Nothing that would interest you," Adam replied.

Peter laughed and faced forward. "I think they're plotting against us. Oh, well, let them. I have them where I want them now."

Adam didn't reply but turned his head and stared out the window. He had to concentrate on their surroundings. If they were able to escape their capture, he needed to know which way to go.

The car turned off the gravel road that led from the clearing onto the highway, and a few minutes later turned onto the road leading to Serenity. Adam kept watch for the spa's main building to come into view, but before they reached it, Bryce turned onto another road leading away from the main building. Then he remembered Peter saying they were going to the barn. A chill ran down his spine at seeing Wes Stratton murdered there earlier. He had no doubt they would do the same with him and Claire if they didn't come up with some way to escape.

Within minutes, the sprawling red barn came into view. Wes Stratton's vehicle no longer sat in front. Only the service vans remained in the same spots where they'd been. As they came to a stop, two men he remembered seeing in the lobby when they'd checked in came through the front doors and waited for Peter and Bryce to get out of the vehicle. The four of them huddled in front of the car and glanced at them from time to time as they carried on an animated conversation.

Every time they looked his way, he frowned. He could tell from the expressions on their faces they weren't discussing some common topic like the weather but were trying to decide how they were going to deal with their two uninvited guests. Claire turned to him and whispered, "What do you think they're saying?"

Adam didn't answer for a moment but kept his gaze riveted on the men. Then he turned his head and frowned. "I can't make it out, but I don't think it's good for us."

"I don't, either."

He leaned closer to her. "I'm going to get us out of this, Claire. I don't know how yet, but I'm working on it."

If his hands hadn't been tied, he would have cupped her face in her hands and brushed his lips against hers. Instead, all he could do was try to keep her hopeful they'd make it out of this alive.

She offered a wobbly smile. "I'm praying you'll find a way."

He returned her smile with a somber stare. "So am I."

The back doors on either side of the SUV opened, and the two men who'd just come outside jerked Claire from the car. As they were pulling her out, Adam glimpsed spiderweb tattoos, not on their hands but spread across their necks. These webs were larger than the others he'd seen, and that meant these men had spent longer periods of time in prison than the others he'd seen.

The thought of being separated from Claire by these hardened criminals made his heart pound with fear. She glanced back at him, and panic seemed to overtake her as she began to scream.

"No! Let me go!" When her feet touched the ground,

she twisted and writhed in the grasp of the men holding her. "Adam!"

The man holding her drew back his hand to slap her but stopped when Adam called out. "Claire, I'm all right! Try to stay calm!"

She stilled at the sound of his voice, and her captors led her to the front of the vehicle where they stopped. Then he heard Peter's voice. "Okay, Knight. Get out of there if you don't want to see your lady friend get hurt."

Without hesitating, Adam crawled from the car and stumbled to a stop beside Claire. The two men glared at her. "Now move."

Claire gulped several breaths before the two of them walked forward and entered the double doors that led into the barn. Once inside, Adam stopped in surprise and let his gaze travel over the spacious interior. He'd expected a dark, musty building that served as a storage place for all kinds of equipment needed to keep a large hotel and grounds like Serenity in perfect operating condition. Instead what he encountered was a sprawling casino that would rival anything Las Vegas had to offer.

He came to an abrupt stop and stared in wonder at the blackjack, poker and roulette tables arranged across the floor and the rows of slot machines and video games with flashing lights that appeared to be scattered throughout the room. Blinking overhead signs identified other areas where games he'd never heard of were played.

Beside him Claire sucked in her breath. Adam looked at Peter, who'd stopped beside him and shook his head. "Willis, haven't you heard that gambling is illegal in the state of Tennessee?"

Peter's eyebrows arched, and he faked a surprised expression. "You don't say. Too bad you're not going to be

able to tell anybody what you discovered." He pointed to
the far end of the building. "Take them to the basement.
We'll take care of them after it gets dark."

One of the men gave Claire a shove, and she stumbled forward. Adam stepped up beside her, and together
they moved toward the rear of the building where they
were guided through a doorway that led into a hallway
with rooms on either side. At the end of the hall Bryce
opened one of the doors, reached inside and flipped on
a light switch.

A staircase led downward to what Adam assumed
was the basement. Bryce motioned with his gun for her
to enter. "Move."

Claire took a deep breath and stepped onto the first
step. Adam followed behind her. At the foot of the staircase, they stopped and looked around. The basement
looked large enough to occupy most of the area underneath the barn. Large concrete columns that reached
from the floor to the ceiling appeared to offer support
for the floor above.

The two men who'd brought them inside each took
Claire by an arm and led her to a column that sat in the
middle of the room. "You, too," Louis said to Adam.

Claire cast one last look at Adam before their captors untied their wrists and forced them to the floor on
opposite sides of the post. Louis and Peter took a longer piece of rope and wound it over their chests and
around the post.

After the men appeared to be satisfied that the two
of them were anchored in place, Peter squatted down in
front of Claire and shook his head. "Look what's happened to you, Claire. All because you wanted to recover

a little bit of money because I jumped bail. You should never have come after me."

"I didn't do it because of the money," she snarled. "I did it because you killed my father."

He nodded. "Oh, yeah. I forgot. That was too bad. He got a little too nosy for his own good. I guess it runs in the family. As does paying the consequences for that family trait."

Adam turned his head, but he couldn't see Claire on the other side of the post. "Leave her alone, Willis. If you want to threaten somebody, take it out on me, not her."

Peter sighed, pushed to his feet and walked around to face Adam. "My, my, aren't you quick to defend this little lady? One would think she's more than just a good friend."

"You can taunt us all you want, but you're not going to elude the police forever. There's going to come a time when you'll have to answer for all the murders you've committed. And when the police find out about your little gambling business, that will only mean more charges."

Peter laughed. "Little gambling business? If you only knew." He turned away and headed back toward the stairs. "Leave them down here. We've got lots to do to get ready for tonight. You take care of them after it gets dark."

Adam watched as the four men trudged up the stairs. Bryce Holt was the last to go, and he gave them one more glance before he flipped the switch at the top of the stairs and plunged the basement into semidarkness.

Before Claire could say anything, Adam spoke up. "Give it a few minutes, and your eyes will grow accustomed to the dark. There's a window at the top of each of the walls, and they're letting in some light."

"I see them," she said. "It looks like the bottoms of the windows are sitting at ground level."

"They are. So they're not a good escape route."

"Do you think we can get out of here?"

"I'm going to try. Don't give up."

"I can't see you." Her voice trembled, and his heart lurched at how scared she must be. He should never have let her come with him today.

"I know," he said, "but I'm here. Are your hands flat against the column?"

"Yes."

"Mine, too. Can you wiggle your fingers?"

"Yes."

"Then try to stretch your fingers toward me as far as you can." He could hear her movement as she struggled to slide her fingers a few inches toward his. After a minute or two, he felt her touch, and they laced their fingers together. "Don't give up hope, Claire. For right now we're together, and that's what's important."

"That's the only thing keeping me going," she whispered as she tightened her hold on him.

Adam's heart pounded at her touch. The uncertainty of what Peter had planned for them still loomed ahead of them, but for now Claire was beside him. And that was all that mattered.

FIFTEEN

Adam strained with all his strength against the ropes that bound him to the column. He didn't think Louis had noticed how he had expanded his chest as the final rope had been placed on him when he was being tied up. Adam could feel the space, but he wasn't sure if he'd allowed enough room to work himself free. He exhaled and felt a small bit of looseness.

But had he left enough space to get out from under the rope around his chest and work his hands free? He needed to try because there didn't appear to be another option.

"Claire," he whispered.

"What?"

"I was able to leave some slack in my ropes. I'm going to try to get free, but it may take some time. I don't want you to give up hope. Just keep talking to me and concentrate on what we're going to do once we're free."

"Okay."

She began to chatter and for the next hour she talked about her parents, the good times she and Jessica had shared growing up and about her life in Nashville. After a while he stopped her. "How are you feeling now?"

"I'm thirsty and hungry. I wish I had the other half of that muffin I left this morning when I figured out you were trying to leave without me."

Adam had worked the rope around his chest several inches up his chest by this time, but he stopped and closed his eyes for a moment. "And I wish you'd stayed at Aunt Sue's. You wouldn't be in this mess if you had."

"But you would," she said. "And I wouldn't want you to be alone. Have you been able to work enough space to free yourself?"

"Not yet, but I'm still trying."

By midafternoon Adam's mouth felt as if it was lined with cotton and his stomach was growling with hunger. He tried to concentrate on something else, but he knew if he was thirsty and hungry so was Claire, although she hadn't mentioned it since earlier. Throughout this whole ordeal she'd been a trouper.

He let his gaze wander around the room and to the windows at the top of the walls. The light that had been filtering in for the past few hours wasn't as bright as it had been earlier, and he wondered if Claire had noticed.

Her attitude during the time since they'd been brought to the casino had amazed him. For the past hour, though, she'd become quiet, and he thought she'd even begun to snore.

She stirred, and he stilled. "Claire, are you awake?"

"I think I was about to nod off. Thanks for waking me. Do you have any idea what time it is?"

"I think it's approaching late afternoon."

"That means they'll be coming for us soon."

The tremor in her voice sent a momentary shock of pain through him. "I don't want you to think of that right now."

"Have you made any progress in getting free?"

"Some, but not what I need yet."

"You can be honest with me. Do you think we're going to get out of here?"

"Claire, I'm still…"

"It's okay," she interrupted. "I know you're trying, but I'm beginning to doubt we're going to make it out of this alive. I've tried to be brave, but we can't ignore the fact that we're in a lot of trouble here. I want to tell you once more I'm sorry for bringing you into this."

He closed his eyes and bit down on his lip. Her voice sounded so wistful and almost as if she'd given up. He grasped her fingers as tightly as he could. "Claire, I'm right where I'm supposed to be."

Her sob drifted to his ear. "Oh, Adam, it's just not fair. I started this, and I should be the one paying the price. Not you. You don't deserve this."

A laugh from the top of the stairs echoed across the room, and the lights blinked on. Heavy footsteps sounded on the stairs.

"But I'm afraid you're right where you need to be at this moment. But don't worry, you won't be for long."

Adam couldn't turn his head far enough to see who was coming down the stairs, but from the sound he knew it had to be more than one person. Claire gasped as the group approached them, and he tried to twist his head to see what had surprised her.

"What are you doing here?" she demanded.

"Just checking on you and your friend, Miss Walker," a man's voice replied.

Adam still couldn't see who had spoken. "Who are you?"

The man moved around to stand in front of him, and Adam's mouth dropped open. He couldn't believe who stood in front of him.

Whitney Hamilton grinned down at Claire before he walked around to face Adam. "You two look a little under the weather, Mr. Knight." He turned to Brian Morrison, who stood right behind him. "Haven't you been seeing to the needs of our guests, Brian?"

Brian smiled and nodded. "Just like you ordered, Mr. Hamilton."

He walked back around to Claire and squatted down to face her. "Too bad James missed you at the bank that day. We could all have been spared what's about to happen."

Claire gasped. "You were the one who had James try to run us down?"

Whitney grinned. "Guilty. But I'm afraid it didn't work out too well with James. After the police officers at the scene told me they'd identified the car as James's, I knew he had to be eliminated. It wouldn't have taken much for the police to break him down, and that wouldn't have been good for any of us."

"How can you talk about killing someone so callously?" Claire asked. "We saw your men murder Wes Stratton, and I suppose you're guilty of ordering the deaths of Lance Morgan and Jonathan Fields, too."

Whitney shook his head and pursed his lips. "Yeah. Lance's and Jonathan's deaths were so sad, but they should have kept their noses out of our business. As for Wes, he knew the consequences of not repaying a gambling debt. He would have gone to the police, too, if we hadn't stopped him."

Claire studied the man standing before her and was bewildered at how someone could talk so casually about causing the deaths of other people. "I don't understand. What are you doing mixed up with these criminals. Do you have a spider tattoo I haven't seen?"

His eyes widened for a moment, and then he shook his head. "No, and I don't intend to ever have one. So that's why we're going to end your snooping into our business tonight."

Claire glanced from Whitney to Brian to Peter, who stood to the side. "It looks like everybody's here to see what happens except Mr. Kendall. When does he arrive?"

Brian and Peter chuckled, and Whitney shook his head. "I'm afraid he's in the dark as far as our business venture is concerned. All he ever did was approve the loan to Serenity, and as long as the payments on the note arrive on time, he's not worried. He might be if he knew how much money I'm feeding into offshore accounts through his bank from our *real* Serenity enterprises in Tennessee, Arkansas and Georgia."

"You have gambling houses in three states?" Claire strained against the ropes that held her. "You can't get away with this forever."

"Maybe not, but by the time anybody finds out, all of us will be gone and living it up on a remote island somewhere."

From the other side of the column, Adam spoke up. "It sounds like you have figured out how you're going to have a wonderful life, Hamilton. Too bad people like Claire's father, Lance Morgan, Jonathan Fields and Wes Stratton won't get to live theirs."

Whitney shrugged. "They shouldn't have gotten involved, just like the two of you shouldn't." He rose to his feet. "I have to go now. This is the biggest weekend of the year. We have high rollers coming in from all over the country, and I don't want anything to cause our special guests any problems."

"So where does that leave us?" Adam asked.

"Not in a very good position, I'm afraid," Whitney answered.

Before he could turn and leave, a female voice called out from the stairs. "Peter? Whit? Are you down there?"

Peter turned and stared toward the sound. "Yeah. What is it?"

Light footsteps sounded on the stairs, and Claire's eyes grew wide as Peter's wife came into view. She didn't glance at Claire or Adam but stared at her husband. "The limo driver just called. The plane bringing our guests from California landed about thirty minutes ago in Memphis, and they'll be here soon. Maria is serving dinner in the guest dining room. We want everything to be perfect for them."

Peter glanced at Whitney. "They're the ones we've been trying to get to come here for a long time. They don't care how much they lose."

Whitney nodded and glanced at Peter's wife, who still stood on the stairs. "Thanks, sis. We'll be there in a few minutes."

"Sis?" Claire and Adam spoke at the same time.

Claire glared at Peter. "So that's the family connection Jonathan Fields thought you had in the bank."

Whitney chuckled. "Yeah, she's my sister. Not that it's going to do you any good to know that." He inhaled and glanced back at Claire and Adam. "Wait until the evening is well under way with the music and the noise level loud before you do anything with these two. Afterward check back with me."

The men turned and walked back up the stairs. At the top they switched the light off, and the darkness that flooded the room seeped into Claire's heart. For the first time she felt despair, and she wanted to cry. She blinked the tears from her eyes and clutched at Adam's fingers.

"Adam, I never believed it would come to this. Is it really the end for us?"

Adam sat up straighter and took a deep breath. "Not if I have anything to say about it. Hold on, Claire. We're getting out of here."

"Can I do anything to help?" she called out.

"I'm going to lean forward and try to loosen this rope around my chest some more. I don't want to hurt you, but it's going to exert some pressure against you."

"Don't worry about me. Just get us out of here."

"Okay. Here goes."

Adam inhaled and pulled forward as far as he could. He exhaled and sank back against the post. "Are you all right, Claire?"

"I'm fine. Try again."

He took another breath, pulled forward, and the rope loosened. "It's getting looser! One more time. Are you okay?"

"Yes. Hurry, Adam."

He gave one last tug, and the rope slipped over his shoulders to hang loosely around his neck. He turned his head sideways and scooted his head out of the loop. "I'm out of the rope. Now it's your turn."

Within minutes he was on his feet and kneeling next to Claire. When he had her free, he pulled her to her feet, and she threw her arms around him. "Adam, I knew you'd think of something."

He closed his eyes and hugged her closer and then released his hold. "We aren't safe yet. We've still got to get out of here."

He took her by the hand, and they ran to the stairs. When they reached the first step, Claire stopped. Adam glanced back at her, and her face had suddenly grown pale. She stared up at the door. "I think I heard them locking the door when they left. How will we get out if it's locked?"

The same thought had been running through his head. "I don't know." He took a deep breath and stared up at the door. "There's only one way to find out."

Adam put his foot on the first step but he froze in place. He suddenly knew the door had been locked because the distinct sound of a lock being turned drifted down the stairs.

Somebody was about to enter the basement.

Claire clamped her hand over her mouth to keep from screaming aloud. Before the lights could click on, Adam grabbed her around the waist and pulled her away from the steps and against the wall that enclosed the stairwell. They huddled against it in silence as the lights blinked on and someone descended.

The person reached the bottom, took a step into the room and stopped. Claire's eyes widened at the sight of Maria, the maid she and Adam had met at Peter Willis's house. She held a plate of food in her hands and turned slowly. Her eyes grew large, and the plate dropped to the floor where it shattered into pieces.

She opened her mouth to scream, but Adam was

quicker. He leaped across the floor, grabbed her and had his hand over her mouth before she could make a sound.

He stared down at her. "I'm not going to hurt you. I just don't want you to alert anyone. Do you understand?"

Claire rushed to Adam's side. "Don't be afraid of us, Maria." She looked down at a sandwich that lay at her feet and the cookies that were scattered about. "Were you bringing us food?"

Maria cast a terrified glance in Adam's direction and nodded.

"Did someone tell you to feed us?" Claire asked.

Maria shook her head.

"Then you were doing it because you wanted to help us?"

Again Maria nodded.

"Then I believe you have a good heart and wouldn't want to hurt us."

Maria frowned and shook her head.

Adam's hand loosened some, but he didn't pull back. "If I release you, do you promise not to do anything that will send a signal to your friends that we're loose?" She glanced from Claire to him before she nodded.

Claire stepped closer. "Then we're going to trust you, Maria."

Adam pulled his hand away from Maria's mouth, and she took a deep breath. "One thing you should know," she said. "They're not my friends."

Adam frowned. "Then what are you doing with them?"

She sighed and shook her head. "I came to Memphis because I wanted to be there for my brother, Louis, when he got out of prison. I got a job working as a maid at one of the hotels and was doing well. Louis and I moved into an apartment, and he told me he had gotten a job working for a man who was trying to help him get his life turned around. He said the man worked in a bank and needed someone to do his gardening, and he said the man's wife needed a maid."

"He was working for Peter Willis?" Adam asked.

"Yes. Louis said it would be a lot easier working for this man's wife than cleaning hotel rooms. I went to see her, and she hired me. It wasn't until later I found out about their gambling business and how much Louis was involved."

"Why didn't you go to the police?"

A tear ran down Maria's cheek. "I didn't want Louis to go back to jail. So I ignored everything I saw. I've begged Louis to get out, but he says it's too late. And to tell the truth I don't think he wants out anymore."

She began to cry, and Claire touched her shoulder. "Maria, why did you bring the food down to us?"

"I heard Mr. Willis and Louis talking about you, and I remembered when you came to see Mrs. Willis. I didn't want Louis to be involved in killing anybody. I decided I'd do something to help you. At the time all I could think about was that you must be hungry, but I think I really came to do more than give you something to eat."

Claire leaned closer. "Are you saying you want to help us get out of here?"

She nodded. "They're going to come for you soon. I think you need to go now. When you get to the upstairs hallway, turn to your left, and you'll see a door with an exit sign over it. Once outside, take the path that leads into the woods."

Adam glanced up the stairs and back at Maria. "Okay, but you need to come with us."

Her eyes grew wide. "I can't. They will kill Louis if I do. You two go. I'll clean up the spilled food and go back upstairs. When they find you're gone, maybe they won't suspect I had anything to do with it."

"Please come with us," Claire begged.

She shook her head. "I can't."

"Claire, we have to go," Adam said. He grasped her hand and pulled her toward the steps.

They'd just reached the staircase when Maria called out. "Wait!" They turned, and she held out a cell phone as she ran to them. "Take this and call the police when you're out of here. Please hurry."

Adam hesitated only a second before he grabbed the phone, stuck it in his pocket, and pulled Claire up the stairs. At the top he opened the door and peeked into the hall. Then he stepped through the doorway with Claire right behind.

Claire glanced back at the basement door and said a quick prayer for Maria's safety before they ran toward the exit. Adam pushed the outside door open and they dashed for the safety of the woods.

SIXTEEN

Adam hoped he wasn't running too fast for Claire to keep up. He looked over his shoulder, and the look of concentration on her face assured him she was managing so far. He slowed when they reached the woods and stopped so they could catch their breath.

"Are you all right?" he asked.

"I'm fine, just worried about Maria. Do you think they'll hurt her?"

"I don't know." He pulled the cell phone from his pocket and tapped in 911.

A dispatcher answered right away. "911. What is your emergency?"

"My name is Adam Knight. My friend Claire Walker and I have just escaped from some men who've held us hostage at the Serenity Wellness Center. We discovered they have an illegal gambling facility set up on the grounds, and they're going to kill us. We need help."

"I'm dispatching officers to Serenity right now. Where is this gambling facility?"

"When the officers approach the main building at Serenity, they'll see a road that turns to the right. Follow that until they come to a big barn. That's the casino."

"I've given them the instructions. Anything else?"

"Yes, you need to notify Bill Diamond at the Memphis FBI office. We discovered these guys have casinos in Arkansas and Georgia, too. They're involved in interstate gambling which puts it under the FBI's jurisdiction."

"We'll let him know. Now I need you to stay on the phone with me until our officers arrive."

Adam was about to respond when he heard the agitated barking of dogs from the far side of the casino. His fingers tightened around the phone as he sprang to his feet. "I'm afraid I can't do that. They're coming after us, and we have to run. Tell your guys to hurry."

With that he ended the call, grabbed Claire by the hand and ran toward the river. "Adam," she cried out. "Are they tracking us with dogs?"

"That's what it sounds like. Can you keep up with me?"

"Don't worry. I can make it."

She'd no sooner uttered the words than her hand slipped from his, and he heard a thud behind him. He jerked to a stop and spun around. Claire lay writhing on the ground.

He dropped down beside her. "What happened?"

"I tripped over an exposed root. I've reinjured the ankle I hurt the other night."

"Can you walk?"

She sat up and rubbed her ankle. "I don't know."

The dogs' barks sounded louder as they echoed on the night air.

He put his hands under her arms and helped her to her feet. When she tried to put her right foot down, she winced with pain and sagged against him.

Adam scooped her up in his arms and dashed in the direction of the river. She looped her arms around his neck and held on as they raced through the night.

With each step he could hear the dogs coming closer. When he was about to think they'd never reach the river, he broke through the trees and onto the path they'd traveled earlier in the day.

He debated which way to go. His car would have been moved hours ago from the clearing, so there was no use in going there. The path to his left seemed the best option. He turned and ran in that direction.

With each step the trail grew narrower, and within minutes the bluff along the right side of the path had dropped into the river. He tightened his hold on Claire as he struggled to keep his footing on the steep hillside. There was no other choice than to go forward, and they descended a few inches at a time. Suddenly he stopped. They had reached a point that he could see what lay in front of them. Instead of the path along the riverbank he'd hoped for, he saw that the trail disappeared into the water. What should he do now?

A loud howl sent a jolt of surprise through him, and he realized whoever had followed the dogs here were so near they would descend on them at any minute. He tightened his hold on Claire, and she glanced back in the direction of the dogs' barks.

The beam of a flashlight swept across them, and a voice from above shouted. "There they are! Get them!"

The crack of a gun split the air, and dirt kicked up from the path a few feet away from them. There was only one thing to do.

"Hold your breath!" he screamed at Claire and jumped headlong into the rushing river waters.

He inhaled a deep breath as he pulled them beneath the swirling waters. The jagged path of bullets striking the water zipped past them, and he struggled to pull them both farther away from where the shots were hitting the water.

They made it into the river's current and he felt Claire being swept out of his grasp, but she managed to loop her arms around his neck. They twisted and turned in the surging water, but Claire managed to keep her hold. She slid around until she was floating behind him but she still held on. For what seemed an eternity they drifted through the torrent before the river calmed, and he pushed to the surface.

The first thing he saw was the moon's light reflecting off the water. The shoreline had changed from the path where they'd entered the river to a small, dirt-covered area flanked by trees. They had traveled beyond their entry point. The dogs' barks sounded in the distance from upriver, and he smiled.

It would take some time for their pursuers to retrace their steps and come along the shore downstream. That could give them time to escape.

The thought had barely entered his mind before his body froze in fear. He turned his head and stared over his shoulder.

Claire had disappeared.

Claire didn't know when her hands had slipped free of Adam's neck. All she could think about was how to survive in the swirling water around her. Her first thought was to give up and let the river take her. She was tired. If she had known her decision to go after Peter Willis would have come to this, she would have backed off before she'd ever begun. But she hadn't, and now she and Adam were probably going to drown. No one would ever know what had happened to them.

But she didn't want to die. She wanted them both to live. And she wanted to tell Adam she loved him, that she always had and always would. He didn't have to return her love, but he had to know he was worthy of being loved. That was what he needed more than anything.

The water calmed, and she kicked to the surface with a new resolve. As she emerged from the darkness below, she looked around, but he was nowhere in sight.

"Adam!" she screamed at the top of her voice.

Only the sound of the river answered.

"Adam!" she called out again.

"Claire!"

Her heart leaped into her throat at the sound of his voice. "Adam, I've over here."

"Keep talking so I can find you!" he yelled.

"I'm here. I'm here. Where are you?"

She heard the water ripple as he swam toward her, and the next thing she knew he had his arms around her and was holding her in a fierce hug. He pulled his head back, looked down into her eyes, then lowered his lips to meet hers.

As she strained upward to greet his kiss, her heart felt as if it was doing somersaults in her chest. This was what she'd wanted for so long, for years. And now it was happening in the middle of a river. She pulled away from him and began to laugh.

The moonlight on his face revealed a puzzled expression. "Is kissing me that funny?"

She shook her head. "No. It's just that you never cease to amaze me. I've waited so long for that kiss and imagined it happening in all kinds of romantic places, but I never pictured us soaking wet in the middle of a river."

He grinned. "Well, Miss Walker, that's only the first of more to come if I have anything to say about it." In the distance the sound of sirens split the air. "I think the cavalry has arrived. I'm tired of treading water. Why don't we get to shore and try to find the good guys?"

She didn't loosen her arms from his neck. "Anything you say, Mr. Knight."

When they reached the shore, he stood up, pulled her out of the water and carried her to the edge of the tree line. He sat her down and then plopped down beside her.

He leaned back against a tree trunk and took several deep breaths. Claire let her gaze drift over him to see if she could spot any injuries he'd suffered, but she saw nothing.

"Are you all right?" she asked after a few seconds.

He nodded. "Just winded." He reached out and grabbed her hand. "I was so scared for a minute there. I thought I had lost you."

"I panicked, too, when I couldn't find you, but we're safe now. Thank you for saving my life now—how many times is it? I've lost count."

He chuckled. "I don't know. But then it seems like I've been looking after you for half my life. I used to get so mad at my mother when she'd make me take you and Jessica to the movies because she was afraid for the two of you to go alone. Or to walk down to the ice cream shop with you."

Claire laughed. "I suppose it was too embarrassing for a cool guy like you to be seen with your sister and her friend."

"I thought so at the time, but things began to change

when you and Jessica celebrated your eighteenth birthdays."

She smiled at the memory of the party their two sets of parents had given them right after they graduated from high school to celebrate their turning eighteen and getting ready for college. They'd rented a ballroom at one of the Memphis hotels and invited all their friends and even hired a band for the night.

Claire sighed as she remembered how happy she'd been that night. "It was a wonderful party, and I nearly died from happiness when you danced with me."

"I was happy, too," he whispered. "But I didn't want you to know. I'd made such a fuss about resenting you for so long, I thought it best to keep up the pretense."

"But why?"

Adam raked his hand through his hair. "I hadn't told anybody, not even my parents, at that point. I'd made the decision to enlist in the military. And you were getting ready to start college. I knew you'd meet new people, maybe find a boyfriend. I thought it was better if I left things as they were."

"And that's the way things stood until you came home a year and a half later."

"Yeah." He took her hands in his and inhaled a deep breath. "I want you to know these past few days, even with all the trouble we've had, have been some of the happiest of my life because you were with me. I fell in love with you years ago, Claire, but I couldn't bring myself to tell you that night at my parents' home. I thought it was better not to saddle you with a guy who probably wasn't going to make it back from combat. So I chose to take what I thought was the easy road and ignore the feelings I had for you. I've been doing it ever since."

"Has it been worth it?"

He closed his eyes and bumped his head against the tree behind him. "Not only was it the hardest thing I ever had to do, it was also the dumbest choice I could have made. I've told myself over and over that I've done you a favor by not telling you, but I died a little bit whenever I heard Jessica talking about a guy you were dating. Then your junior year in college when she said you were serious about someone you'd met, I resigned myself to the fact that I'd missed my chance."

"Why didn't you tell me this after my engagement was broken?"

"I don't know. Ignoring you had become a habit by then, and I thought it was best not to try to revisit past history. Everything changed when I walked out of that woods the other night and saw you lying on the ground. When I realized how close you'd come to being killed, I nearly went out of my mind."

Tears of happiness filled Claire's eyes. "Adam, I…"

"It's all right, Claire," he interrupted. "I understand how much I hurt you, but I was happy when you said you'd like for us to be friends. You don't have to love me like I love you. I just thought it was time you knew. You can go back to Nashville knowing that you weren't the only one who's been unhappy because of my actions. But although I love you with all my heart, I don't expect anything in return."

She tightened her fingers on his and leaned over to stare into his eyes. "Oh, Adam, if you only knew how I've longed to hear those words from you. I've loved you for so long I can't even remember when I didn't. After you were sent back into a war zone, I tried to forget you, but I have never been able to."

His eyes grew wide. "Are you saying…?"

"Yes, I'm saying I love you, too."

He leaned toward her but stopped before their lips met. He reached up and slicked her wet hair back from her face. "One more thing, Claire, not only do I love you, but you've shown me the way to heal my battered heart with the love God has to offer me. Thank you for doing that."

Joy like she'd never known flooded through her as his words burrowed into the secret places of her heart that had seemed empty for years. She'd only been half a person, alone with no one. Now she had Adam, and for the first time in years, she felt whole.

SEVENTEEN

Adam stopped at the edge of the woods. The October night had grown cooler, and Claire shivered in his arms. He pulled her closer to him and stared down at all the activity in front of Serenity's casino. Bill Diamond stood beside a car parked at the barn's entrance as he talked with a sheriff's deputy.

He inclined his head in the direction of the men beside the car. "The man with the deputy is Bill Diamond. He's the head of the Memphis FBI office and a good friend of mine. Let's go talk to him."

Claire stirred in his arms. "What a time to meet one of your friends. I must look a mess."

He frowned and gazed down at her. "Yeah. You look like you fell in the river."

She laughed and swatted his arm as they started toward the barn. Bill looked up and yelled out as they approached. "Adam! I've got men out looking everywhere for you."

Adam chuckled. "Sorry to be so long about getting here, but I figured you could handle things. Tell me what's been going on?"

"We raided the casino, and I think we have everybody who was involved. The guys who were following you even came back, and they're inside with the rest of those we've detained. But I was getting worried about you. Where have you been?"

"It's a long story, Bill, but we're safe, except Claire's ankle is hurt and she's cold. She needs to get to a doctor."

"We can take care of that right now." He turned to the deputy. "Can you transport this young lady to the hospital while I talk with Adam about what they discovered here tonight?"

"Sure," the man replied. "Put her in the passenger seat and I'll take her right away."

Claire shook her head. "I don't want to go without you, Adam."

"It's all right. I'll fill in the police and Bill about what's happened here tonight, and then I'll come to the hospital. I won't be long."

"But…"

Bill opened the car door, and Adam slid her into the seat. When she was settled, he pulled the seat belt and leaned over to fasten it. He leaned close and smiled. "Please don't choose this time to become your independent self again. I love you and want you to be taken care of."

Her eyes softened, and she cupped his cheek with her hand. "I love you, too."

He brushed his lips across hers. "I'll see you in a little while."

When he closed the door, he watched the deputy until the car had disappeared in the distance. Then he turned back to Bill. "Okay. Catch me up on how things have gone since I called the police."

Bill motioned toward the front door. "Let's go inside

where it's warmer. You're soaking wet. I'll get someone to bring blankets from the main house."

They walked inside, and Adam stopped to take in the scene before him. At the back of the room police officers stood guard over a group of Serenity employees who sat on the floor. Some of the women were crying while the men stared into space. Sitting in the middle of the group, Adam spotted Brian Morrison, Louis, Maria, Bryce Holt and the two men who'd helped take Claire and him hostage.

Men and women who he assumed to be Serenity's guests sat around the room either being questioned by law enforcement officers or waiting their turns. A man at the side of the room kept yelling at the officer that he wasn't saying a word until his attorney arrived.

Bill led him into a room off the main gambling floor that he recognized right away as an office. Three officers, their hands resting on their holsters, stood guard over Whitney Hamilton, Peter Willis and Peter's wife.

Peter flashed a look of hatred at Adam. "I wish I'd killed you the other night in Mississippi."

"I'm glad you didn't, Willis. Now I'll get to see you pay for the crimes you've committed." He glanced at the other two. "Along with your wife and friend here."

Whitney glared at him. "We'll see about that. We have influential friends, and it'll take a lot to convict us."

"I don't think we'll have any trouble, Mr. Hamilton," Bill said. "The FBI has been aware of businesses believed to be involved in money laundering for a long time. In the past few weeks we've been able to track their deposits to several banks, and the one you work for is one of them. And I believe your sister here is on the board of another on the list. You've had quite a ride with your casinos bringing in money, then laundering it through banks you control before sending it to offshore accounts. We shouldn't have any trouble linking all of you to these crimes."

Whitney's face turned red, but before he could speak, another officer stepped into the room. "Sir, we're ready to transport these prisoners to jail."

Bill nodded. "Good. Get them out of here."

As the three were led from the room, Peter glanced back at Adam. "Tell your girlfriend I'm coming after her when I get out."

Adam walked over to Peter, stopped in front of him and shook his head. "Somehow I don't think that will scare her. With all the murders you've committed, I don't think you'll ever see the outside of prison again." Then he smiled. "But I will tell her she's going to get the money refunded that she forfeited because you jumped bail."

The officer pushed Peter forward, and they walked out the door. Adam turned around and shook his head. "Peter Willis is the worst guy I've ever tracked."

Bill's cell phone rang, and he put it to his ear. He listened for a moment and nodded. "Good. We're in the main office." He ended the call and motioned for Adam to sit in one of the chairs. "That was one of the officers who's bringing some blankets for you. While we're waiting, why don't you catch me up on all that's happened?"

Adam sank down in the chair and groaned. He hadn't realized how tired he was. Now all he wanted was to see Claire and assure himself that she was all right, then go home and take a hot shower before going to sleep. But first things first. He had to give his account of events to Bill.

He rubbed the back of his neck and yawned. "My involvement in this case started when I was hired by the Bond Squad to track down James Lester, a guy they'd posted bail for."

For the next fifteen minutes he poured out his story as Bill listened. From time to time he asked a question before letting Adam proceed. When Adam got to the part about Maria's help, he stopped at a knock on the door.

A young officer entered with two blankets in his hands. "I'm back with what you wanted, sir."

Bill rose and took the blankets from the man and handed them to Adam. "Thanks, Officer Truett."

Adam wrapped one of the blankets around his shoulders and draped the other one from his waist to his feet. They offered a bit of warmth, but his wet clothes stuck to his body and sent a chill through him. He pulled the blankets tighter and directed his thoughts back to Maria and how she had helped them.

"Mrs. Willis's maid, Maria, put herself in danger when she helped us escape. She did it because she wanted to do the right thing. Do you think that will help her?"

"I don't know, but I'll put in a good word for her. You and Claire can, too."

"Good." Adam took a deep breath. "We thought after we were out of the basement we would be safe, but that wasn't the end of it."

Bill listened quietly as Adam told the rest of the story of trying to escape the dogs tracking them, of plunging into the river and frantically searching for Claire. He ended by saying, "When I spotted you in front of the casino, I knew our troubles were over."

Bill shook his head when Adam quit speaking.

"That's some kind of story, Adam. I'm glad you and Claire are both safe, and I appreciate the service you've done us by uncovering an illegal gambling empire. Not only have the ones behind this bilked untold numbers of people out of their money, but they've sent millions, and maybe more, out of the country to offshore accounts where they'll be free of our tax laws."

Adam smiled. "Thanks, Bill, but we didn't start out with that in mind. All we wanted was to bring in two guys who had jumped bail. I have to say, though, these were the toughest two I've ever encountered. I hope I don't come across any more like them."

Bill laughed. "Don't count on it, buddy. There are guys out there all the time who think they can break the law and get away with it. Local law enforcement doesn't always have the funds for officers to track down the ones who've jumped bail. I'm thankful we have an agency like your family's to go after them for us. Keep up the good work."

Adam nodded. "I will. Now, if you don't need me anymore, I'd like to get to the hospital to see how Claire's doing. Do you think one of the officers could give me a ride?"

"I think that can be arranged. Come on."

They rose from their chairs and walked back into the main casino gaming room. Most of the employees who'd been under guard earlier were now gone, probably transported to the police station. Officers still questioned those who'd been guests.

Bill stopped beside the young officer who'd brought the blankets earlier. "Officer Truett, Mr. Knight needs a ride to the hospital where they took Miss Walker. Can you help him out with that?"

The man smiled. "Sure. Can I take you anywhere first and let you change clothes?"

Adam turned to Bill. "What hospital did they take her to?"

"Green Haven, just north of here," Bill said.

"That's good. I stayed at my aunt's house there last night." He glanced back at the officer. "How about dropping me at her house so I can shower and change. Then I'll borrow her car to go to the hospital."

Officer Truett nodded. "No problem."

Bill followed them as they headed to the front door of the casino. "We'll try to find out what they've done with your car and get it back to you, Adam. In the meantime, tell that young lady we appreciate what she did, and I look forward to seeing her again under better circumstances."

"I'll tell her, Bill."

As they walked toward the car, Adam stared up at the moon and remembered how glad he'd been to see it when he'd emerged from the dark waters of the river. A shiver ran down his spine at the memory of what he and Claire had experienced tonight, but then a feeling of peace washed over him as the truth hit him. God had been watching over them in that river tonight, just as He'd been there all these years Adam had denied Him.

No matter how much Adam had protested His existence, He'd stayed close and brought him back to Claire and a change in his life that made him happier than he could ever have thought possible. As he stared up at the moon and stars in the night sky, he prayed silently that God would make him worthy of the great gifts he'd been given.

* * *

Claire sat on the table in the exam room and waited. Adam would come. She knew he would, but what could be keeping him? She'd already been here several hours, and she hadn't heard a word.

Then her heart raced. He was coming down the hall. She would recognize his footsteps anywhere. She held her breath, and then he walked in the door. He stood there for a moment and stared at her as if he couldn't take his eyes off her.

She reached up and smoothed her matted hair, which was now dry. "I must look a mess."

"You're the most beautiful thing I've ever seen," he said.

Before she could reply, he rushed across the room and grabbed her in his arms. "Are you all right?" he asked.

"The doctor says I'm fine. And I am, thanks to you. I never would have made it alone, Adam."

He held her away from him and stared into her eyes. "No, I'm the one who wouldn't have made it. Thank you for being there with me and keeping me going even when I wanted to give up."

"Did I do that?"

"You did. There have been times in the past when I would want to give up on something I was doing, and I'd think of you and I'd keep going because I didn't want to appear to be a failure in your eyes. So you see, you've been prodding me on for years and didn't know it."

She laughed. "I'm glad. Does that mean I can keep doing it in the future?"

A small frown creased his forehead, and he stared down at her hand as he wrapped his around it. "That's what I want to talk to you about."

The look on his face frightened her. A few hours ago he had said he loved her. Maybe he'd thought about what he said and wished he hadn't spoken so quickly. Maybe he was about to tell her what she'd suspected for a long time. He wasn't the type to settle down with one woman. She tried to pull her hand away, but he held her tight.

"Claire, we said some things when we came out of the river we need to talk about."

Her heart pounded so hard that she could barely breathe. "What do we need to say?"

He cleared this throat. "We need to decide where we go from here."

"Wh-where do you want to go?"

He shook his head. "It's not important what I want. I want you to be happy. You told me not too long ago that you wanted to go back to Nashville to your old job and your old life. If that's what you want, I don't want you to feel you owe me anything."

"Do you want me to go back to Nashville?"

He jerked his head up and stared at her. "No. I want you to stay here with me. But I won't stand in your way if you don't want the same thing I want."

She smiled and leaned forward. "What do you want, Adam?"

His gaze traveled over her face. "I want to marry you. I love you, Claire."

She pulled her hand free of his and looped her arms around his neck. "I don't want to go back to Nashville. I want to stay here and marry you, too."

His eyebrows arched, and his mouth pulled into a big grin. "Do you mean it?"

"I do."

He dropped to one knee and gazed up at her. "Then,

Miss Walker, will you do me the honor of becoming my wife and making me the happiest man alive?"

She laughed. "I will, Mr. Knight."

He jumped to his feet and pulled her to him. When his lips touched hers, she knew she was right where she was supposed to be. In Adam's arms.

When he pulled back, she stared up at him with a teasing look. "Since I won't be going back to my old job and since I plan to close the bail bond business, it looks like I'm unemployed."

"Don't worry. We'll find you something."

She reached up and trailed a finger down his cheek. "Since I'm going to become an official member of the Knight family, I think I'd like to join the Knight Agency as a bounty hunter. I think we'd make great partners."

A shocked expression covered his face before he shook his head. "No way are you going to put yourself in danger again like you have the past few days." He pulled her closer and trailed kisses down her face. "But I do have an idea."

"What?"

"We've been shorthanded ever since our receptionist quit. Dad's been filling in some, but he really wants to retire. I think you'd be perfect there. That way I could see you every day at work as well as at home."

She smiled. "I'll think about it and let you know."

"You always have been independent," he said as he brought his lips closer to hers.

Before she could respond, he captured her lips in another kiss, and independence was the last thing on her mind.

EIGHTEEN

Two weeks later Claire sat behind her desk in the reception area of the Knight Agency and sighed in contentment. The events of the Peter Willis hunt, as it now was being called by Adam and his family, seemed as if it had happened in another lifetime. Things had certainly changed for her since she started on the manhunt that would change her life.

She stared down at the engagement ring sparkling on her hand and then to the surroundings of her office located in one of the most desirable buildings in East Memphis. Sometimes she thought she needed to pinch herself to make sure everything she was experiencing was real.

The door to the hallway opened, and Jessica hurried in. She stopped beside Claire's desk and dropped down in a chair. "I overslept this morning. Has Adam asked where I was yet?"

Claire shook her head. "No, he's in his office. He calls me every five minutes, but he hasn't asked about you yet."

Jessica grinned. "I didn't think I'd ever see my brother so crazy in love." She reached over and squeezed Claire's hand. "Thanks for not giving up on him. I knew you'd get together some day."

Claire laughed. "Well, you knew more than either of us did."

"I had more faith, I guess. But tell me, how are the wedding plans coming along? We only have a few weeks left before the big day."

"I know, but everything's worked out. It's not going to be anything fancy, just a private wedding in the sanctuary of your family's church. And then a dinner at the Peabody. The only people coming are your family and Aunt Sue. We want her there."

Jessica tilted her head to one side and directed a stern look at Claire. "You have to quit referring to them as 'my' family. They're yours now, too."

"I know. It's just so hard to believe. I have to keep telling myself it's real." She paused for a moment. "Jessica, I know there hasn't been anybody in your life for a while, but if you'd like to ask someone to come to the wedding with you, that would be great."

Jessica pushed to her feet. "Nope. No one I'd want to ask. I'll be content to be the bridesmaid and make your day the happiest it can be."

Claire started to respond, but the phone rang. She glanced down and frowned when she spotted the number on caller ID. She rolled her eyes and groaned. "It's Adam's cell phone. He calls me all the time."

Jessica covered her mouth to keep from laughing out loud. "Well, see what he wants."

Claire picked up the phone. "The Knight Agency. This is Claire. How may I help you?"

Adam's voice drifted into her ear. "Claire, would you come in here, please? I need you to take some dictation."

She arched her eyebrows. "Adam, you know you don't dictate to me."

"Oh, right," he said. "I forgot you are Miss Independence. Fortunately for me, though, your last name is going to be changing soon to Knight. So would my beautiful fiancée help her intended out and come into his office?"

She giggled in spite of herself. "All right. Since you put it that way."

She hung the phone up and sighed. "He wants me to go to his office."

Jessica laughed and headed toward her office. "Then go on and take him out of his misery. I'll see you later."

Claire walked down the hallway toward Adam's office, opened the door and stuck her head inside. He was seated at his desk staring at his computer screen. "I'm here, Adam. What do you want?"

He didn't look up but motioned for her to come inside. "I need to show you some sites on the internet."

"What kind of sites?" she said as she walked around and stood beside him.

"Hotels. Places that sound good for a honeymoon. We haven't picked out a place yet, and I wondered if you'd like to choose."

She clapped her hands together and let out a shrill laugh. "How wonderful! You hadn't said anything, and I was afraid you couldn't get away from work. And then I have just started here."

He smiled up at her. "Don't worry. The boss will give you the time off. Now, let me show you what I've found."

She pulled up a chair beside him and sat down to study the pictures. "I can hardly wait to see what you've found."

He brought up the first site. "Here's one on the beach in Maui in case you want to do two weeks in Hawaii."

"Um, that's nice."

He glanced at her and pulled up the next one. "And here's one in London, if you want to go to Europe. We could spend a week in London, then go on to Paris."

"Sounds good."

He sighed and pulled up the third one. "Or how about San Francisco. It's a beautiful city."

"It is," she said.

He sat back in his chair and stared at her. "None of these seem to be what you want. If you could choose, where would you go?"

She leaned over and grasped his hand. "It's sweet of you to want to please me with the perfect vacation, but as long as I'm with you, that's the perfect honeymoon."

"I feel the same way about you." His eyes sparkled with love for her, and a warm rush flowed through her. After a moment he cleared his throat. "But that doesn't solve the problem of where we're going."

She laughed. "You choose."

"Okay." He pulled up another site and turned the computer screen so she could see the picture. "How about this?"

Her eyes grew large at the picture of the rustic cabin that filled the screen. The mountains in the background could be none other than the Smoky Mountains. The Realtor's information covered the bottom of the screen.

"This is beautiful, and it's perfect. Do you think we could rent it?"

He shook his head. "I don't think so. The new owner is very picky about who stays there."

She turned to him. "How do you know?"

He smiled. "Because I bought it yesterday."

She gasped and fell back in her chair. "You did what?"

"I remembered how I used to hear you talk to Jessica about how you loved the Smokies and someday you were going to have a vacation home there so you could visit anytime you wanted. I found this one for sale and thought it would make a great wedding present. What do you think?"

Tears filled her eyes. "You remembered hearing me say that?"

He stood, pulled her to her feet and put his arms around her. "I did. I remember a lot of things about you." He smiled and tucked a strand of hair behind her ear. "I know your favorite candy is jelly beans, and your favorite holiday is Thanksgiving. I remember how you would follow my mother around the kitchen and question her about recipes and how your eyes crinkled at the corners when you laughed at my father's corny jokes. I also know that you have the most amazing ability to help people who are suffering from problems in their lives. But most of all I remember how you felt in my arms the night I danced with you at your eighteenth birthday party and how I never wanted to let you go."

"Oh, Adam," she whispered. A tear slipped down her cheek, and he brushed it away with his thumb.

"I also remember how you wanted to help me that night in my parents' kitchen, and how I hurt you. I'm going to spend the rest of my life making up for how I acted when I was young. I love you so much, Claire."

She cupped his face in her hands and stared up into

his eyes. "And I love you, Adam. I can't wait for our life together to begin."

"Neither can I," he whispered. "Neither can I."

* * * * *

Dear Reader,

I'm excited to share with you *Fugitive Trackdown*, the first story in my new Bounty Hunters series. Although the story is about the hunt for an elusive fugitive and the danger-filled journey of Adam and Claire who are tracking him, it is also about faith and trust in God. Adam has denied the existence of God for years and comes to understand what the Bible tells us in Galatians 3:26—For ye are all the children of God by faith in Christ Jesus.

If you haven't opened your heart to God's love and put your trust in Him, I hope you will. God is waiting for you to invite Him into your life.

Sandra Robbins

PROTECTION DETAIL
Capitol K-9 Unit • by Shirlee McCoy
A congressman is shot, and Capitol K-9 Unit captain
Gavin McCord promises to protect all in the marksman's path.
When a foster mother and children are added to the target list,
Gavin must bring the culprit to justice before he strikes again.

STRANDED
Military Investigations • by Debby Giusti
Colleen Brennan is trying to bring down a drug trafficking
scheme. But when a wild twister traps her in an Amish town,
she must rely on Special Agent Frank Gallagher to get out alive.

HIDDEN AGENDA • by Christy Barritt
To find his father's murderer, CIA operative Ed Carter enlists
the help of nurse Bailey Williams. But now they're both in the
sight line of a cold-blooded killer...

UNTRACEABLE
Mountain Cove • by Elizabeth Goddard
As search and rescue volunteers, Isaiah Callahan and
Heidi Warren never anticipated being lured into a trap set by
robbers. Now they'll need to outwit their captors—if they
can forge through deadly icy terrain first.

BROKEN SILENCE • by Annslee Urban
When someone wants Amber Talbot dead, her ex-fiancé—and
detective on the case—must keep her safe. Patrick Wiley
agrees to put their history aside...to help the woman he hasn't
been able to forget.

DANGEROUS INHERITANCE • by Barbara Warren
Macy Douglas returns to her childhood home searching for
answers. When an unknown attacker determines to keep
Macy from digging up her family's past, officer Nick Baldwin
must uncover the ruthless criminal's identity before they're
sent six feet under.

_____

**LOOK FOR THESE AND OTHER LOVE INSPIRED BOOKS WHEREVER
BOOKS ARE SOLD, INCLUDING MOST BOOKSTORES, SUPERMARKETS,
DISCOUNT STORES AND DRUGSTORES.**

LISCNM0215

REQUEST YOUR FREE BOOKS!
2 FREE RIVETING INSPIRATIONAL NOVELS
PLUS 2 FREE MYSTERY GIFTS

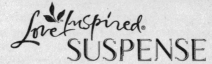

Love Inspired®
SUSPENSE

Michael Jeffries was dead, and there wasn't one thing Capitol K-9 Unit Captain Gavin McCord could do about it. It seemed inconceivable, impossible, but it was true. Michael had been a good guy, a great attorney. Fair-minded, reasonable and determined to always see justice done. Now he was gone, shot down in the prime of his life.

That hurt. A lot.

Gavin snapped a picture of the bloodstain on the pavement at the rear of congressman Harland Jefferies's mansion. He'd already had the evidence team collect samples for DNA. He knew they'd find DNA matching Michael Jeffries and his father. Like Michael, Harland had been shot by a small-caliber handgun.

Unlike his father, the young lawyer hadn't survived.

Sad. All the way around.

Gavin knew and liked both of the men, but he couldn't let his emotions get in the way of the investigation. He snapped another picture, glanced around the scene. The DC police had been the first responders, and several officers were huddled together discussing the case. He knew most of them. He'd worked as a DC police officer for ten years before taking the job Margaret Meyer had offered him. It had been an opportunity he couldn't pass up, one that he hadn't *wanted* to pass up.

Glory shifted beside him. The three-year-old shepherd was too well-trained to stand before she was told to, but it was obvious that the excitement of the crime scene was making her antsy.

"Be patient," he said.

"McCord!" one of the DC officers waved him over.

"What's up?" he asked, approaching Dane, his gaze jumping to the bloodstained concrete where Harland had been lying. Michael's body had been found a few feet away.

"One of my men found something near the tree line. I thought you might want to see it." Dane held up an evidence bag with a bright blue mitten in it. "Thing was clean as a whistle. Not a leaf on it. Not a stick. Not a speck of grass covering it."

"It looks like a kid's mitten," he said. They had a possible witness!

Don't miss
PROTECTION DETAIL by Shirlee McCoy,
available March 2015 wherever
Love Inspired® Suspense books are sold.

LISEXP0215

SPECIAL EXCERPT FROM

Love Inspired

A young Amish woman yearns for true love.
Read on for a preview of A WIFE FOR JACOB
by Rebecca Kertz, the next book in her
***LANCASTER COUNTY WEDDINGS** series.*

Annie stood by the dessert table when she saw Jedidiah Lapp chatting with his wife, Sarah. She'd been heartbroken when Jed had broken up with her, and then married Sarah Mast.

Seeing the two of them together was a reminder of what she didn't have. Annie wanted a husband—and a family. But how could she marry when no one showed an interest in her? She blinked back tears. She'd work hard to be a wife a husband would appreciate. She wanted children, to hold a baby in her arms, a child to nurture and love.

She sniffled, looked down and straightened the dessert table. And the pitchers and jugs of iced tea and lemonade.

"May I have some lemonade?" a deep, familiar voice said.

Annie looked up. "Jacob." His expression was serious as he studied her. She glanced down and noticed the fine dusting of corn residue on his dark jacket. "Lemonade?" she echoed self-consciously.

"*Ja*. Lemonade," he said with amusement.

She quickly reached for the pitcher. She poured his lemonade into a plastic cup, only chancing a glance at him when she handed him his drink.

"How is the work going?" she asked conversationally.

"We are nearly finished with the corn. We'll be cutting hay next." He lifted the glass to his lips and took a swallow.

Warmth pooled in her stomach as she watched the movement of his throat. "How's *Dat?*" she asked. She had seen him chatting with her father earlier.

Jacob glanced toward her *dat* with a small smile. "He says he's not tired. He claims he's enjoying the view too much." His smile dissipated. "No doubt he'll be exhausted later."

Annie agreed. "I'll check on him in a while." She hesitated. "Are you hungry? I can fix you a plate—"

He gazed at her for several heartbeats with his striking golden eyes. "*Ne,* I'll fix one myself." He finished his drink and held out his glass to her. "May I?"

She hurried to refill his glass. With a crooked smile and a nod of thanks, Jacob accepted the refill and left. The warm flutter in her stomach grew stronger as she watched him walk away, stopping briefly to chat with Noah and Rachel, his brother and sister-in-law.

Annie glanced over where several men were being dished up plates of food. She then caught sight of Jacob walking along with his brother Eli. The contrast of Jacob's dark hair and Eli's light locks struck her as they disappeared into the barn. They came out a few minutes later, Eli carrying tools, Jacob leading one of her father's workhorses.

As if he sensed her regard, Jacob looked over and locked gazes with her.

Will Annie ever find the husband of her heart?
Pick up A WIFE FOR JACOB to find out.
Available March 2015,
wherever Love Inspired® books and ebooks are sold.